MW00872730

Ulyssis Revisited

A novel by Katheryn Lovell

AuthorHouse™
1663 Liberty Drive, Suite 200
Bloomington, IN 47403
www. authorhouse. com
Phone: 1-800-839-8640

This is a work of fiction and should be read as such. The characters,thoughts and opinions expressed are the products of the author's imagination."

First published by AuthorHouse 2/20/2009

ISBN: 978-1-4389-2868-5 (sc)
ISBN: 978-1-4389-2867-8 (hc)

Cover design: by K. Poulin
Author Picture: Karen Cossman

Printed in the United States of America
Bloomington, Indiana

This book is printed on acid-free paper.

To my "Ulyssis" ... who captured my imagination along with my heart

Acknowledgements

Like all projects, many people had a hand in the conception, design and support in the final production. I need to thank all the "patients with the keys," mostly "retired' from SSH; Elois, Carolyn, Stan, Matt, Dr. G. and all the members of the treatment team who have earned my respect and love for their compassion and professionalism. And, of course, my dear friends Kay, Pat and Deenie. We have nurtured and maintained strong friendships in spite of all the insanity! A special thought for Margaret who is, sadly, no longer with us. But I imagine she is still taking good care of everybody in Heaven! I am truly honored to have had the experience of learning, working and most of all, laughing with you.

I am grateful to have had the great fortune to have been aided in my research by my neice Chati, who rounded up additional first hand accounts of the war and translated them as well. What a gift to have support on both sides of the Atlantic!

My "cheerleaders," my academic friends and colleagues at Thomas Nelson who were excited about the book from the start and whether they realized it or not, offered me wonderful support. Thanks to the college administrative team of Debbie Bedosti, Ruthie Simon and Mike(Boris)Bruno who's daily inquiries of my progress spurred me on, especially when I was needed it. And a special thank you to Prof. Vic Thompson who gave generously of his time and energy and offered wonderful suggestions to the project. Again, thank you. And to my good friend Karen Cossman, who in addition to "prodding," donated her photographic talents.

Thanks and appreciation go to my children:sons Chris and Josh and daughter Kim, who continue to tolerate my 'chicken checks' with patience and good humor. Kim's artistic book cover design beautifully captures the essence of the story. Thank you, daughter! You have all made me one proud Mother Hen!

And finally, thanks to all the people, on all sides of Spain's Civil War who were impacted by this cruel event and were willing to share their experiences.

It is much too easy to inflict harm on others when we see them as "The Other" ; not fully human. May we remember and honor those who suffered in this conflict and try to grow beyond our petty political differences and learn to embrace each other as fellow human beings.

PREFACE

One always questions the true impetus behind one's decision to actually write, finish and publish a book. It has been, at times, an albatross, a frustration, a challenge. But as I researched and listened to these stories over the years, I came to know so much more about the lives of those involved. And I have to admit that I began to view their dreams and struggles in a far more sympathetic and heroic light. Simply: these stories need to be told.

Manolos's journeys begin early as a child of war. Sadly, there is very little literature about the subject, from any era and one can only speculate about the many possibilities for this phenomenon. Do we as adults minimize children's experience? Or disbelieve their memories? Or could it be that we simply want to believe that time will erase any unpleasant memories? Unfortunately, our wishful thinking is just that. Our brains store much more than we realise and powerful events, especially traumatic ones, are usually seared into our memories along with the emotions. I think it would benefit all of us if we listened more to the experiences, especially those of the children.

The title, Ulyssis Revisited, came about as I thought about the struggles of leaving the familiar to wander the world looking for meaning and especially that elusive thing we call "home" . He had absolutely no idea of where he would end, just a fearless drive to get there. I describe him as a person of great spirit and greater passion and it is that combination that propels him forward toward success and, at times, really compromising situations. I like to think of him as a composite of Homer's Ulyssis and Cervante's Don Quixote with a little bit of Don Juan mixed in.

The myth of the Greek Ulyssis describes him as a wanderer. For many years after the Trojan War, he endures several adventures as he wanders about the Mediteranean Sea, finally returning home to his beloved wife and to claim his throne and rightful place.

Don Quixote's quest, a blend of idealism and courage(not to mention a few delusions) strikes me as akin to Manolo's; remaining strong and steadfast in spite of overwhelming odds of failure.

Zorilla's Don Juan Tenario had become the most familiar image of Don Juan. That Don Juan is mostly portrayed as a arrogant womanizer engaged in an unending search for sexual gratification. But there is another version of Don Juan that better reflects Manolo. Lord Byron's epic poem presents Don Juan as being extremely naive and not the pursuer, but the pursued. It is Byron's subject that reminds me of Manolo's romantic adventures.

Like many Americans, my father's people originated in Scotland. However, no family members can recall any stories of their immigration to Boston. I knew my "Gampy" Andrew, a retired Custom House clerk, but his battle with 'the drink" left him incapable of thinking about much other than himself and his basic needs. It almost seemed as if he had blotted out any memories, pleasant or otherwise in his destructive quest for chemical solace.

No stories from him remain but many stories about him.

There is a peculiar phenomenon that often occure in families. Somehow, grandchildren end up closer to their mother's parents than their father's; curious but true. So it was with my own family of origin. Although they did not know each other in County Galway, both of my mother's parents immigrated from Ireland, to Boston. I know little of my grandfather as he died when my mother was twelve. But I do know that he served in World War One and later became a police captain in Boston.

My "Nana" sailed alone to Boston as a young teenager. A married brother and his family was forced to return to the family farm and since she was lower on the pecking order; a girl, she relinquished her bed to them. A case of literally "no room at the Inn." Her family decided that she needed to seek her fortune in America. Sad as she was at leaving, she accepted the reality of her situation and decided to make something of her life. Had she stayed in Ireland, by her own admission, she would have faced a dull life of helping her "Ma" take care of a household of brothers until she, perhaps, married. ; essentially a life of servitude.

She made the best of her difficult situation and faced her New World with optimism and her Faith. As her namesake, I sometimes like to entertain myself with the idea(or delusion) that I may somehow carry some of her determination in my DNA.

The stories that she told were precious few and even her own children could not recall much information. It didn't take long before she abruptly ended a tale in tears: it was just too painful to continue when she remembered leaving her "Ma and Pa." It was much easier and very human to do so as many did; build a wall of silence to avoid the searing memories.

Speaking with many other families of Celtic origins, this silence was very common and frustrating for those of us who were trying to piece together some of the ancestral past. So much of history, real people's experiences. has been lost forever. But it is not a simple loss of a few tales(so what) but the loss of people's wisdom and knowledge. We must remember the words of the Spanish born philosopher, George Santayana: "Those who cannot remember the past are condemned to repeat it." As humans, we cannot afford to ignore this piece of wisdom and yet we continue to do so.

Now, Albacete, Spain is the home of my familia Espania. Warm, engaging and extremely hospitable, they immediately welcomed me into their home and hearts and we happily converse in our particular brand of Spanglish. Mi Espe and Santo Jaime (and dear Pepe) are people muy fabulosos!

Bur as wonderful as my visits have been, I came to notice something as familiar as it was disturbing. Like the Celts. the people of Spain do not speak about the recent past. They can readily discuss Spain's history during the Golden Era but shy away from delving into the devastating events that occurred during the first half of the twentieth century. Although the country endured over three years of a horrific civil war, very few people are comfortable talking about it.

Even more astounding, this attitude of silence is apparently promoted by the Roman Catholic Church and the country's politicians. And it happened almost seventy years ago.

It has been said that History is written by the winners. But it is vital for a true and fair understanding of any conflict to have a holistic view; the view of the vanquished as well as the victors. The experiences of all sides need to be told. My many professional years as a nurse, psychotherapist and college professor have taught me that all wounds, whether physical or emotional, cannot heal until they have been addressed, cleansed and brought to the light to properly heal. Denying or ignoring or keeping them undercover and secret just makes them more painful and ultimately, destructive to the individual. And this applies to a society, as well.

Luckily during my research, I was able to obtain some eyewitness accounts and I appreciate the painful recollections that my prodding may have elicited. I have tried to stay faithful to those memories. In digging up some authentic accounts, I was fortunate to engage the help of my neice, Chati, as most of those accounts are dying out with the survivors; the youngest are in their eighties. Again, remember Santayanas's earlier truth: "Those who cannot remember the past are condemned to repeat it."

Too often, we who have not left our homelands do not fully appreciate the tremendous ordeal it truly is. All immigrants share at least one trait and that is courage. Every human being has the right, out unalienable right, as our treasured Declaration of Independance states to "Life, Liberty and the Pursuit of Happiness." Honestly, how many of us have any appreciation of the depths of those rights?

Mark Twain's quote:" Courage is resistance to fear, mastery of fear-not the absence of fear" truly exemplifies my concept of courage. It is not a denial of the risks and dangers or our inner reactions to them. Fear of the unknown and anxieties about failure are natural human emotions. It is that wee bit more of belief, of effort or time that singles out, marks one as having courage. And it is those people we deem "extraordinary." The rest of us fall short or give in to our fears and anxieties, keeping us in the realm of the "ordinary."

And so my image of Manolo suggests a universal immigrant's tale:an archetype and powerful symbol of one's own life experiences and it's ultimate value is shaping just who we are and will become.

And as for my Nana, I still smile when I think of one of her rare stories. To her dying day, she believed in Leprechauns; even claimed she saw one as a girl in Ireland. And you know? She just may have.

"We must be willing to give up the Life we've planned so as to have the Life's that 's waiting for us"
Joseph Campbell

"Courage is the resistence to fear...mastery of fear- not the absence of fear"
Mark Twain

Chapter One

The boy sprinted out the door with such determination that he barely heard his mother calling, "Manolo...Manolo...be careful. And hurry! I'll be waiting here for you!"

"Si, Mama..... I'll hurry back.... don't worry!"

The bombing had already begun. His father, Fernando, had already taken his two sisters to the bomb shelter, leaving his wife, infant son, and Manolo behind. Nine year old Manuel "Manolo" Sanchez had already picked up the mantle of "man of the house," at least in his mind. Based on his father's behavior, it was the logical conclusion made by the boy and today's events were further proof.

Manolo had overheard the women's conversation earlier and understood that his mother had stopped producing any milk for the infant Jaime.

They spoke about other women whose breast milk had dried up due to the tension and stress felt by everyone. That left only one option:someone had to get some milk, cow or goat, whatever was available. This was just another one of the many casualties of the war.

"I won't let Mama be humiliated like Senora Goya. I'll make sure Jaime gets milk, on my honor." He had been shocked, listening to his parents discussion at last night's dinner table. The discussion had centered on a family that lived in the outskirts of Albacete. Manolo sometimes played soccer with one of the sons but knew nothing of the family troubles and his friend had said little about his family since the death of his father. The Goya boy seemed quieter than usual but it would have been rude of Manolo to pry into another's family affairs; that much he had learned from both teachers and his parents. He remained curious like any young boy but would wait until he was informed.

After all, his own family was experiencing major problems and best to remain focused on those.

Senor Goya had been recently killed defending a Republican stronghold in the north. A poor farmer, he had made the decision to defend his beliefs of a better life should the Socialists win. Should that happen, he could hope for justice and prosperity for his family and all who worked hard. He too, was tired of slaving; eeking out a meager existence while the Church and aristocracy did next to nothing, but tradition and birthright ensured wealth and leisure. Did God really favor those with wealth and power as the Church had taught? What about the teachings of Jesus? The ones about sharing and helping your neighbors? He had enough of words. Words kept them poor. Words couldn't feed a family.

Leaving his wife and eight children, two of them mere infants, he joined the battle truly convinced, as he had told his family, that he would be home before the harvest. The older children would have to work a little harder to maintain the farm until his return. Yes, It would be very difficult but he reminded them that everyone must sacrifice for the noble cause.

With the death of her husband, Senora Goya sank into dispair. Working even harder to ward off depression, she became ill. But in spite of back breaking labor, she and her children couldn't manage the farm and very quickly, their meager supplies and food dwindled to nothing. Two of the children, the older infant and a three year old girl soon succumbed to starvation and without some charity from neighbors, the others would soon follow.

Between the anxieties of war and poor nutrition, Senora Goya could not produce the vital breast milk for her infant's survival and the baby would join his siblings in death. And given the ongoing politically based rancor between the village families, the situation looked hopeless.

But, as in any crisis, someone decided to forgo the pressure of politics and aid a fellow suffering human being. A woman whose husband was also at a battle but in the opposing Franco's forces, had just given birth. Mother and infant were healthy and she was producing an abundance of milk. She was well aware that she and her neighbor were technically enemies, and that she would incur much wrath from other villagers should she behave otherwise. But watching a baby slowly starve to death, in her mind, was more of a sin. Deciding that she would help, she walked to the poor woman's home and nursed her baby as well as her own. Months of literally feeding her neighbor paid off, for the baby not only survived, but flourished.

"Funny," thought the boy" That baby has two mothers- his real mama and his "milk" mama. But not in our family, all Jaime needs is one."

Manolo ran along Albacete's side streets making a beeline for the dairy. He was confident, as only nine year old boys are, of his mission's success:bringing milk back for Mama. Thinking that his father should be the one providing for the family didn't even cross Manolo's mind. Fernando had, long ago, lost his son's respect.

"Hey boy! Hey. over here. The bombs are coming." People were scrambling to shelters all over the city. Manolo ran on. If his brave Mama could stay and wait for him to return, he must run on. The whistling of the German Stutkas began. Manolo, as did every Spaniard with any sense, knew that this terrifying sound signaled destruction and death for anyone unfortunate enough to be near the drops. "I can't believe Hell could be any worse than this.I don't care what the priests say..." His thoughts and pace were rudely in-terrrupted by a huge explosion; the first of many to come.

The explosion hurt his ears, but the boy knew it wasn't close enough to do any real damage to him. The temporary ringing in his ears was expected.

He thought of his friend, Eduardo who had been too close to one of the German bombs and had lost all hearing and permanently. Like any boy his age, he was longer on bravado than wisdom. "I'll just run faster, that's all." Finally reaching the Dairy, he fell into dismay. It was deserted and there was no sign of the owners, even though everything else looked to be in it's usual place. Manolo realized that he was all alone and had been for at least the last twenty minutes." They must have gone to the shelter." From previous visits, he knew which bottles to grab.

"I should leave a note for them. I wouldn't want them to think I'm stealing and Mama would be furious, and Papa ?I don't even want to think about his reaction!"

At that moment another bomb hit the pavement on the next street, jolting Manolo and the counter of bottles. The bomb drops were getting closer.

"I'll come tomorrow and explain...I'm sure they will understand... I just hope Mama does."

As quickly as he had come, the boy retraced his steps back to his mother.

The bombs had stopped but the people were still in the shelters. The air was still.

No sounds could be heard exept Jaime's wails, and they, too, abated with the milk. The stillness seemed unearthly...it was almost as if they three were the last people on earth. Thankfully, the "all clear" siren rang.

The crisis over, the people of Albacete returned to their homes and businesses. Paloma and Pilar ran into the Posada's kitchen to find their mother and brothers safe. Their mother looked at them and asked where their father was. "Oh, Mama, you know Papa... once it was all clear, he sent us home and went to The Cafe to play his dominos. He said he'll be home for dinner.'

Silent, Dona Elena 's face displayed her showed her disappointment and irritation.

Pilar, the youngest sister, knew her mother was stung by the news but she wasn't going to lie for her father. What would be the point? It was just Papa's way. She was aware of his "quirks" but he was her beloved Papa and she had long ago accepted him as he was.

She was well aware Mama would make no comments, after all, it wasn't a woman's place to question her husband's behavior but body language often betrayed deep feelings. Although the girl loved Papa, she was acutely aware of the ongoing "drama" between her parents, and she decided maintaining a quiet ignorance concerning the subject best served her interests. Best to simply accept one's God given role in life, as any challenge brought too much conflict and inevitable heartache. She didn't understand or share her older brother's expectations in life and in her opinion, he suffered from an overly sensitive nature.

"Like the women say; men are alot of trouble!"

Manolo's reaction was predictable and he took no pains to hide his emotions.

He was livid.

"I guess playing dominos with his friends is more important than seeing his family safe! Nothing new there." he spat.

"Manolo! I won't hear you talking about your father so. I've told you many times:He is still your father and you WILL respect him!"

Manolo adored Mama but didn't share her views on the subject of Papa.

His relationship with his father was practically nonexistant. Any physical affection was reserved for his sisters, not him. He never remembered his father showing care for his mother and that was a sore spot. Mama was an angel, second only to the Virgin. How could her own husband not adore her as Manolo did? Papa was a complete mystery and try as he may, he simply could not understand him.

So many things about his parents, and their relationship confused him.

Why did the girls sleep in one room while he, Jaime and Mama in another?

Everyone was crowded; everyone except Papa. Papa had his own room and a a big bed all to himself. And why was Papa the only family member to have the comfort and safety of a mosquito net?All summer, everyone complained about these small biting demons. The insects made life miserable and at night, sleep was nearly impossible.

"Why does Papa have a net and we don't, Mama?," asked Manolo scratching yet another bite.

"And why do you ask me that everyday? As the head of the home, your father is entitled to be comfortable. Now stop complaining."

"So what are we..... ?"

"Ooooooo, cabezone!" But Dona Elena was half hearted in her remonstration of her son. She, also, wondered the same.

But he would show him the respect demanded of any son; that he could do But like him? love him? No, that was too much to ask. "I don't think Papa likes me much either, so I'll try to avoid him, best I can."

As he thought further, The only real attention that his father bestowed upon him had happened a few years ago. The Corrida was Papa's first love; Dominos the second. Religiously, he followed the career of his favorite matador or torrero named Barrera. He has been so impressed by the man that he had named the family dog after his hero.

Fernando had taken his obsession with the matadors a step further and decided that his son would train as a matador at age six. Having a toreador as a son would surely bring great honor and prestige to the Sanchez name.

The only honor that would surpass that would be the priesthood, but not in Fernando's eyes. The toreador was the very symbol of power, and above all, respect.

Manolo had little interest in anything to do with the bullring but realized it was a chance to earn his father's love and respect. The little boy would go along with Papa's plans. And who knows, maybe he would learn to like it!

Fernando enrolled him in the local academy for weekly lessons and outfitted him in a miniature" Suit of Lights" . Decked out as a professional matador, in miniature of course, the boy felt silly but he saw something in his father's eyes, something that he rarely saw: pride.

"Now, you look like a man!" Fernando beamed. "Just the future for a son of mine.... for a Sanchez! Think of the glory, Manolo, the respect!... Why, if you really work hard, you could be better than even Barrera!"

"Si, Papa......"

One day father and son were at the bullring hoping to catch one of the famous toreros practicing his art. They watched as each artist displayed the elegant movements of the cape including the "Veronica" . These daring sweeps of the cape were named after the Catholic Saint Veronica who, the story goes, supposedly wiped the face of Jesus Christ at his crucifixtion.

"Mira.. Look! See that girl ? Look how fearless she is. She's walking right up to that bull...Look! The animal is bowing to her. What courage! Don't tell me my son has less courage than a mere girl?"

Humiliation rose in Manolo. No, he must show no fear. He couldn't be shown up by a girl! The whole scene was causing quite an uproar as the girl continued to pet and caress the huge beast. Amazing! But Manolo's shame lifted when he heard some men discuss the scene.

"It really isn't all that uncommon, you know." stated one man.

"Aw, come on! I don't see you jumping in the ring and petting it!" replied a second.

"Ahhhh, You don't know who she is! She's the daughter of the bull's breeder and has raised that beast since it was a calf! Even bottle fed the monster! Now he thinks she's his mama!"

Laughing, the two men continued their conversation concerning the other bulls. In amazement, he turned to his father to share the story. Fernando's scowl indicated his mood as he, too, had overheard the men. "Bah, what do they know anyway!" Clearly, the story had no impact on Fernando's ambition for Manolo's future in the bullring.

Dona Elena had distinctly other ideas regarding her first son. Elena spent more time with Manolo so she knew his interest lay in education, in learning and not in a life of vain and glory as a toreador.

"Fernando. Why push the boy? It's obvious he is doing this to please you and not for himself! Can't you see that? Por favor...please, stop trying to live your dreams through Manolo!"

"You pamper him too much, Elena.... Look at him! Strong, sturdy, smart, but all you women fuss over him like he's a prize turkey! He needs to be more of a man! More physical! No one respects a mama's boy!"

But for all his efforts, Manolo showed little apptitude or interest and eventually even Fernando had to admit that fact. He was not pleased.

"Bah.... a mama's boy, that's what you are! So go run along...go to Mama!"

Since that episode, he had little to say to his son. It was clear to the boy that his father was disappointed in him, but what could he do? He hated the stupid suit. What he liked was learning...especially about history. That's what stimulated his imagination and made him dream. History!Now that was exciting!

For his part, the boy found his father's behavior confusing. It was painful to see his mother ignored. And the pompous way his father strolled around the town, acting and dressing as if he were a

Lord or something! The most annoying part was his father's absolute refusal to engage in any employment making his disdain for "work" very public. Why, that was for ordinary men, not someone with his pedigree. He was a Sanchez!It was almost as if family was just an after thought. It was an embarrassment for the boy. He was proud of Papa's heritage but why couldn't he work like everybody else's father?

Dona Elena, not her husband managed La Posada, the Inn along with a few paid servants. Grateful that they had stayed on to help, she treated them as old family friends. She was the one constantly meeting with vendors, supervising the help, and welcoming guests. Those who knew Elena had nothing but praise for the woman.

Without hesitation, she offered a sympathetic ear and "forgot" the bill of fare for a family in need. Unlike her husband, she had earned respect. of the town's people. It was acknowledged the Sanchez household was unusual, a wife running a business with little help from her husband but no one dared to actually make any comments to Fernando. That would be disrespectful to him, as head of the house. But that didn't stop the gossip mills from grinding out their constant buzz.

At his retirement, Manolo's maternal grandfather Ginez had given the Inn to Elena, the oldest child. Although a girl, she was the brightest and most efficient of his three children. Possessing a pleasing personality, she ran the Inn efficiently but humanely. Each of her brothers could have succeeded their father but neither was interested in running the Inn. Another brother, Manolo, had been the heir apparent but he had died tragically of an illness years before at the age of twenty. This loss had been so devastating that his parents had insisted that the first born male grandchild of the surviving siblings be named Manolo. Dona Elena had dutifully named her first son Manolo. As it happened, she and her sisters-in-law were pregnant around the same time. So just a few months apart, the extended family was blessed with three Manuels... the three Manolos.

For many years, Ginez was aware of her of his daughter's domestic situation. Since her marriage, her family had grown to include two grandaughters and an eight year old grandson, Manolo. He was fully aware that her relationship with Fernando was tense. His son-in-law had proved to be a weak, ineffectual husband and rumors of his philandering activities had reached him.

His visits to Valencia pained him as he saw his daughter working hard, and his son-in law essentially loafing about, boasting of his "connections" . He prayed that she and her husband would accept his offer of relocating and managing La Posada. Why, if they would come and run the Inn, he would retire and have her and the grandchildren about. As the Inn was only one of his investments, he could virtually give it to her. He had made enough money for a comfortable retirement and although he didn't quite trust Fernando, having them in Albacete would enable him to keep an eye on the situation.

The boy's thoughts turned to his cousins; the two "other" Manolos. They seemed to get along with their fathers and both his uncles were always kind to him. But try as he might, he couldn't figure it out. He made attempts to speak with his Tios about his father but came away with the same...nothing. Reticent to involve themselves in another man's family affairs, they advised the boy to discuss the issue with his father. After all, the father was the acknowleged head and final authority in Spanish families, no one disputed this fact. But Manolo had approached Papa, several times, in fact and only to get the same results: sarcasm or out and out rebukes and rebuffs. So the boy continued with his usual strategy:avoidance. But that did nothing to alleviate his pervasive sadness about his Papa.

Politically, the Sanchez family remained divided. Fernado's sympathies sided with the monarchy and aristocracy, the conservative "Whites" His daughters, although less political, aligned with their father. Elena just wanted her family to live in peace. But Manolo was Leftist through and through. His active imagination naturally leaned toward the idea of Rebels fighting for a just and free Spain. In his daydreams, he had joined the Communists and bravely fought for this honorable dream. Once in awhile, when he was feeling some bravado, he would march around his home singing the Communist anthems that he had learned in school. Feeling powerful, he knew it infuriated his father to no end, but other than dirty looks, no attempt would be made to silence him.

Paranoia was rampant these days and it was dangerous to be seen as other than Pro-communist. People were "disappearing" only to be found days later with a bullet in their head. IF they were found at all. Even family was suspect, as politics and ideals turned into blood feuds. Tension was mounting in the entire country.

Manolo's mother would ask him to stop the singing, knowing her son's behavior was partly due to his sentiments. She was all too aware of the growing distance between her oldest, beloved boy and her husband. Manolo's sisters, however, were fearless.

Deeply devoted to their father, as most daughters are the world over, his sisters challenged their brother. Whenever he started to sing the Internationale, the Communists's banner anthem, they belted out the Fascist song; Cara al Sol.

Their parents, used to this daily display of sibling rivalry, did their best to block out the rising cachophony until the inevitable chases began. It didn't matter who began chasing whom, it was embarrassing for each parent to witness his or her usually well behaved children running through the Inn screaming.

"Cabeza de Mierda!" taunted Paloma

"Estupido!" added Pilar.

"Putas!" countered their brother

"Dios Mios, hijios! Stop!" Their parents knew the siblings would eventually tire themselves and settle down but their parents remained mortified at their behavior.

"It doesn't make any sense. I try to be good. Why doesn't he care about Mama...or me?And no one tells me why! Maybe Papa's sick!Maybe he's loco! But he acts like he's better than everyone. I wish, just for once, I wish I could see somebody teach him a thing or two.... boy, that would be something....."

Manolo's rocky relationship with his father was just one small piece of his world, albeit an important one. His world, and that of all of Spain had begun to make no sense at all.

"In Spain, the dead are more alive than the dead of any other country in the world."

Federico Garcia Lorca

Chapter Two

The seeds of Spain's Civil War had been sown much earlier than the actual declaration made on July 18, 1936. The country had been leaning "left" for a while as had most of Europe. The Russian Bolshevics has taken the country from the Czar Nicholas and had executed him as well as entire family. Systematically, the peasants gained power and exiled or executed the ruling class. No matter the society, human beings almost always followed the same course and eventually, the oppressed became the oppressors.

Germany was following suit. In the 1920s and 30's, Germany's leftist goverment failed to provide prosperity for it's people and the people were ripe for a strong, charismatic leader who tapped into their dreams of superiority. This leader, Adolf Hitler, focused Germany's ills on the marginalized:homosexuals, gypsies and, of course, the Jews. The people found it easier to blame others for their own shortcomings; unfortunately a universal tendency.

Italy, too, was undergoing similar changes and a new dictator emerged: Mussolini, and political turmoil was to start in another European country:Spain.

Rebellion and strikes were frequent in monarchist Spain as the society became further polarized. People chose political stances but it was not as simple as the conservative monarchist Right versus the liberal, left leaning Republicans.

Unrest, bombings and strikes continued as the society became further chaotic. Jose Antonio Prima de Rivera, the son of the previous dictator, began his political career as a moderate but began to embrace the Right, establishing the Falanges.

Now a Republic, the King and his wife Victoria Eugenie, a granddaughter of England's Queen Victoria, were exiled to Italy.

The Conservative "Whites" were divided. Monarchists known as "Carlistas," wanted a strong King, dreaming of the "Old Glorious Spain" . The Roman Catholic Church demanded her piece of the political pie as did the Fascist military. Why even the color "white" suggested purity and virtue!

By 1936, it had all bubbled to a head.

The military generals directed General San Jurjo to lead a military coup; a revolt on July 17, 1936. He, however, died in a plane crash which left them with their second choice:General Fransico Franco in charge. July 18th, 1936 is generally accepted as the beginning of the Spanish Civil War.

A short, stout man, he did not suffer fools gladly. Fully aware that he had not been the first choice, he was determined to succeed. His time, exiled in the Canary Islands, had been fruitful as he not only maintained his supporters and troops, but added many more both inside and outside of Spain. The Foreign Legion and many Moorish fighters were just waiting for some action. At his word, these battle hardened soldiers would quickly muster and take back their county from the perceived enemy. Germany provided transport by air and sea for the army's march from Gilbraltor to the Spanish mainland.

But Franco had another ally that proved as effective as his soldiers: The Church. The Roman Catholic Church was already hard at work prortraying anyone with Socialist leanings as misguided and enemies of The Church. The Church's "rotweiller's," The Holy Office worked tirelessly amassing information on Spain's citizens. The Holy Office had been previously named The Inquisition and still maintained most of it's policys and ideas but the name change did nothing to diminish it's power or ability to instill fear, as every devout Spaniard believed; the Church held the ultimate power:the power over one's very Soul.

Franco traveled to Gibralter to plan his first battle. His crack professional troops, the Foreign Legion and Moors, had seen much warfare and were battle hardened and eager to deploy. Confident of victory, the first attacks would entail crossing Gibralter into the Spanish mainland into Andalucia and another "Reconquest" of Spain would begin.

The next several months brought world attention to the conflict. Spain's national poet and open critic of Fascism, Federico Garcia Lorca, was murdered by the Fascists. The "official" explanation given was he was a homosexual; a degenerate and traitor according to Fascist dogma.

Another event, the seige of El Alcazar in Toledo, brought daily newspaper and radio broadcast around the world. Colonel Moscado held the stronghold for several weeks until the Reds had tunneled beneath and blew it up. As a show of support, Franco diverted a march on Madrid only to arrive to rubble. Moscado emerged and famously stated, "Mi General...sin novedat en El Alcazar. My General, no news of the El Alcazar."

The rest of the world watched and waited as the drama unfolded. A "NonIntervention Pact" was signed by the other countries but Portugal broke it almost immediately enabling German and Italian support to Franco. France, siding with Reds, opened her borders but only sporadically; not enough to really make a real difference. Even Britain's conservative Neville Chamberlain openly sided with the Fascists Hitler and Mussolini and referred to them as his "friends'.

Mexico was the only country to fully support the Republicans. And it must be noted that Texaco supplied gas and oil, on credit, to Franco's forces. Although the United States populist mostly sympathized with the Republicans, the US conservative right wing members of Congress and antiCommunists supported the Fascists.

The Republican goverment, meanwhile, sent much of Spain's gold reserve (about 578 million dollars) to the Soviet Union to purchase war supplies.

Eventually some were sent.

One of the more horrific episodes occurred on April 26, 1937. Hitler's scientists had developed a new airplane firebomb that had not been tested.

Anxious to do so, Franco agreed to sacrifice a small city in the Basque province, a city known to be fiercely independant and against Franco. Because of their "troublemaking," they were highly expendable. The destruction would send a chilling message to any other group that had separatist ideas.

April 26, 1937, Market Day, was chosen as the maximum number of people and animals would be on hand; a better target. Without warning, the city, it's people, animals and buildings were mostly obliterated. Initially, the Fascists were proud of the accomplishment but as the world heard of the atrocity and registered condemnation, they soon concocted a story trying to shift blame proclaiming the Reds had bombed their own people. Pablo Picasso immortalized the city in his famous painting named simply after the city:Guernica.

The Republicans were joined by a group of young international volunteers, some who came out of a sense of outrage while others; for adventure. But all shared the same ideals of a free and fair Spain. An International Brigade was formed led by a Frenchman, Andre Marty. The most famous section, consisting of American volunteers, was known as the "Lincoln Brigade" in honor of Abraham Lincoln; the American Civil War President.

Their numbers included writers and journalists Americans Ernest Hemmingway, Robert Merriman and Frenchman Andre Malraux as well as Englishman George Orwell, just to name a few. It was largely through Merriman's reporting that the English speaking world kept current on the progression of the war. Several years later, this same Merriman became doubly famous; initially, as an heroic war correspondent and later as the main character in one of Hemmingway's novels.

The decision was made to train and house this "Lincoln Brigade" in a small city; Albacete which was centrally and strategically located approximately one hundred and severty five miles from Spain's capital of Madrid.

By 1938, Franco informed Hitler, who was busy invading neighboring countries, that he would not end the war peacefully. Even more disturbing, amnesty would not be granted to anyone who had opposed him.

The Vatican officially recognized Franco's goverment and began a "cultural cleansing." Any regional language such as Catalan was banned. No divorce or civil marriage were allowed and all children born must be named after Catholic saints. Only literature, books, art that had a Nationalistic or Catholic theme were accepted. Even Goya's masterpiece "The Maja" was considered pornographic. The country was, essentially, thrown back centuries.

In spite of it's viciousness and sectarian violence, there were some displays of reason. The mayor of a tiny village, Alatoz (population six hundred) declared," No one will kill anyone as long as I am mayor." And for the duration of the war, it was so. The inhabitants had their differences but managed to transcend the violence. Each day, as they all listened to the radio for reports, any battle was celebrated; no matter who won. And this community of fatalists remained unharmed.

On April 1, 1939 (April Fools Day), out gunned and outmanned, the Republicans finally surrendered to the Fascists. Although it was known as the "Franco Government," General Francisco Franco ruled as the dictator until his death in 1975.

As bad as those war years were, life was to get even harder, especially for those with "Red" sympathies. Retributions for slights, real or imaginary, ruled the society for many years. Many were exiled, imprisoned or executed. The Fascists supporters, naturally faired better with opportunities; such are the spoils of war for the winners. But that is not to suggest the "Reds" were the only ones who suffered. Atrocities were committed by both sides, and ultimately, many thousands of people died.

Shortages of just about everything, except misery, was the norm; food, fuel, medical supplies and money. All of Spain suffered under Franco, as an Allied blockaid lasted ten years from 1945-1955 during the "Cold War" years. Between that and the Civil War, Spain was essentially in ruins for almost twenty years. The blockaid was finally lifted when the United States, under Eisenhower, offered-Franco a better deal for an alliance than had Russia's Stalin.

Franco did allow King Alphonso's son and heir, Juan Carlos, to return to Madrid for a Spanish education. The boy returned, but his parents remained in Portugal and Juan Carlos remains King of Spain today.

It has been said that Spain's Civil War was actually a "dry run" for World War Two. And I believe most historians would hesitate to disagree.

Chapter Three

Fernando Sanchez was the third child born to an upper class, elitiest family. His family line reached back centuries and the Sanchez name was well respected. Like most members of that class, children were expected to have a modicum of education, mostly the boys, and be sustained by the family wealth.

The most one did was oversee one's land and servants; the people who labored long and hard for their 'lords" . Fernando's family was no exception. No exception, that is, until his father ran off and left the family. Senora Sanchez had little money of her own to care and raise four small children as her husband essentially left his wife without finances or respect. She had fallen in the social structure and being the aggrieved party made little difference.

The wronged woman had no choice but to "farm" her children out to be raised by respectable middle class, childless couples.

The youngest had remained with her but Fernando and his sisters were sent to separate households. The children held the belief that the situation was temporary and dreamed of being reunited again as the patrician Sanchez family but this was not to be. They all stayed in the adopted homes for the rest of their childhoods. Fernando was twelve years old when he began his new life with the Navarros.

Senor & Senora Navarro were pleased to accept the boy and truth be told, felt some honor as well, knowing the boy's family. But they quickly realized that any expectation of additional help in the family leather business was a non starter. Fernando quickly disabused them of that notion. Trying to help, they gave him a home in which his expectations would continue. They asked nothing of him in the way of helping with chores and the boy certainly did not offer. Such an absurd thought for a person of his quality!

The older couple hoped the sullen boy would make friends, settle into his new surroundings and come to care for them However, there was little evidence of that ever happening. Still, they freely gave him spending money and granted every request no matter how much it compromised their wants or need. In short, Fernando never accepted his reduced social status and harbored resentment toward the Navarros and blamed his parents for his embarrassing situation. He spent his adolescence and early adulthood in leisure as he followed the bullfighters, played dominoes, chased girls as well as any other pleasures he could think of.

Fernando never forgot that he was from a well-to-do, elite family. It never occurred to him that times were changing and he felt no empathy for the "lower class" ; in his mind, anyone who soiled his hand by actually having to work was inferior. He believed himself to be a superior person and anyone, especially young ladies, should be grateful for his attentions. After all, he was a Sanchez and far above most of them.

Initially, he had accepted Senor Navarro's training and education and by the age of sixteen had developed a reputation as highly skilled in the grading and selection of leather hides. Yet, once he developed the skill, he refused to put it to use. He held the satisfaction that a few large leather firms had offered him employment, and unsolicited at that! But no amount of pleading or cajoling could budge him from his decision:he would not work. It was simply beneath his station.

His belief in his own superiority was apparent with his treatment of any laborer and his gruff manners and sharp tongue quickly made enemies. Except for his small band of like-minded ne'r-do-well friends, he was generally known as around town as a pompous layabout.

Many years later, after he went with the Navarro's, his adopted mother fell ill. Since she could no longer help with the family business and Fernando was told that he needed to "go find a woman" to work. Senor Navarro was getting old and need help in the shop. He had, long ago, accepted the fact that Fernando would never lower himself to assist so the request translated into: "go marry a good woman and bring her here to work." It was not lost on him that he needed to do as he was asked. He certainly wasn't going to work in the shop and someone had to, somebody needed to make money for him. And Senor Navarro had made it very clear that the funds were drying up. As he was now in his late thirties and ready to marry, he grudgingly complied. He thought it couldn't be too difficult to find a suitable wife. Any woman would surely be impressed.

In the small town of Gandia, there was no shortage of eligable young women ready for marriage. With his patrician air, dapper clothes and proud manner, he cut quite handsome figure, at least on the surface.

In 1920's Spain, as in much of Europe, courting was done "from afar."

Ladies would stand on the wrought iron verandas and speak to their prospective suitors from this safe distance. Once interest was shown, the man or his designee contacted the prospective bride's parents, and an agreement was made. The couple was rarely left alone, as this would have been a serious breach of ettiquette. For women, being known as "pure & virginal" was crucial to a good match and less virtuous females following no such restrictions were labelled as" unsuitable matches," or worse.

Unfortunately for both parties, getting to know one's prospective spouse before the match was rare. Sometimes, these matches evolved into true love and affection but many a young lady (or gentleman) found the reality of the marriage far different than expectations prior to the betrothal. For faithful people, Catholic Spain offered few options:wives could seek solace in The Church or direct their prayers and petitions toThe Virgin.

According to strict religious dogma, The Virgin Mary had suffered more than any human woman and could understand a woman's plight. She could bring solace as she brought the woman's prayer requests to her son, Jesus Christ. The best one could hope for was a strong faith in The Virgin and The Church, for divorce was not an option.

Husbands, also bound by the no divorce dictum, could ignore any problems or visit the local brothel; a common practice and a silent reality for it was well known that The Church protected the prostitutes while preaching against the practice.

A smooth talker, Fernando focused on his well known family of origin, not the Navarros and minimized his present situation. After all, it was only a matter of time when society would restore his family honor and his new wife would share in his rightful place. Surely any reasonable young lady could see what a superior person he was. He had money, but like most members of his class, no job. He believed himself quite the "catch" and worked to instill that belief in others.

Bored with his small town's females, he traveled to nearby Albacete to continue his search for a suitable mate. She must be attractive, smart, and healthy. After all, she would be the one working once he brought her back to the leather shop.

Chapter Four

Before her marriage to Fernando, Elena was known in the town, as a beauty. She was the eldest and only daughter of Don Ginez and his wife, but in spite of having the misfortune of being born female, she proved herself like her father in most ways. Her quick mind, sound judgment, and love of learning made her a natural for business. She had other dreams, however, she longed to be a teacher.

A voracious reader, she devoured any written material available and loved to debate ideas with anyone who was willing. Even her brothers were wary to debate an issue with her, knowing she would have been well prepared. This one wasn't content with women's gossip; she wanted discussions of substance.

But her academic dreams would never materialize. Both brothers made it clear that they would not be following their father in his businesses. Their mother was not even considered since Ginez felt his wife too frail and prone to hysteria.

She could barely manage their home, never mind a business!

In addition to the Posado, Ginez ran a lucrative contracting firm that, at present, took most of his time and energy. It was necessary for a family member to manage the Posada, and his daughter was the obvious choice. He trusted his daughter's intelligence and social acumen. Although sympathetic with his daughter's hopes and dreams, he firmly believed family obligations came first and especially in these unstable times. It was best to have all his family together when the clouds of war were hovering about.

Although heartbroken that her dreams of teaching would never materialize, she was a dutiful daughter and accepted her father's wishes. She turned her energies into making the business flourish, making him proud and her books would give solace and company when she was alone.

The Don chuckled to himself as he remembered a particular time when his daughter proved more than a match for him. At age sixteen, Elena had disrespected her mother and the verbal shouting match between the two had resulted in leaving his wife hysterical and Elena stomping out of the house. He could not, for the life of him, figure out the actual cause of the battle as both of his ladies remained sullen and mute. His wife, however began to beg him for satisfaction for her perceived injury. After all, wasn't he the "man of the house"?

Don Ginez wracked his brain for a solution to the dilemna. He didn't share his wife's outrage, yet he believed children should be obedient to parents. He had to reaffirm this sense of family order, so Elena must somehow be punished. That was the trick:how to do so?

The Don sighed as he approached his daughter and informed her of his decision. She was to stay in her room for twenty four hours and with no meals and only water to drink. Knowing how resourceful she was, he locked her in her room from the OUTSIDE. At the end of this "exile" she could resume her duties.

Her acceptance of this punishment without protest puzzled him, but he could now face his wife and a return to normalcy.

It didn't take long for Elena to open her second floor balcony window and call down to the servants. She paid them to hoist up food, especially her beloved chocolate. The servants knew enough to stay quiet about the entire transaction. This was a family matter but no harm at keeping the Don in the dark; the whole enterprises was a big joke to them. They adored the family, especially Elena and they readily agreed to be part of the ruse.

Her passion for chocolate was well known and she kept a locked box of the treats in her bedroom, for "emergencies". Anytime she felt lonely, angry, sad, or anxious, she knew some candy would soothe and calm. It really was the best medicine, she found, and would continue this practice throughout her life.

After the twenty four hours had ended, the Don knocked on her bedroom door. He expected Elena to be anxious to come out and to show some contrition for the whole ordeal. What he got was very different.

"Elena! Come downstairs now, all is forgiven!"

"Thank you, Papa...but no...I think I'll stay awhile longer."

"But Elena, come.We have a nice dinner prepared. You must be hungry!"

"Oh, Papa, I'm praying now for my sins. I think another day of fasting will make my soul strong. Don't worry Papa, I'm fine."

Believing his daughter had become more pious, he returned downstairs. He decided to walk around the Inn to check on his supplies before he had dinner but as he looked across the courtyard, he watched as one of the employees hoisted a basket of food to his waiting daughter.

Ginez hadn't dreamed she would pull this trick but he wasn't surprised, just another example of his daughter's resourcefulness.

"Are you ready to come to dinner now?" he asked as he gazed up at her balcony. He stood laughing and shaking his head.

"Si, Papa. But only if you don't tell Mama. Please?I'm sorry, honest!" But her smile betrayed her. She was sorry to have been caught by her beloved Papa. Actually, she had enjoyed the whole game. It had been a break from the everyday routine and a little exciting, as well!

Years later, the Don would fondly remember this incident. It was in great contrast to her decision to marry. There, she seemed to have forgotten her intellect and judgment. Clearly, some other variables were at work there but then, he thought, We rarely use judgement in affairs of the Heart.

Elena settled into a comfortable life assisting her father with the business. She was quick to learn the accounts, and her gentle way with people endeared her to them all. She treated the servants like any of her aquaintances ; those she liked were old friends but those she didn't still had her respect. Elena was her father's daughter when it came to the "class hierarchy" . Because of her role at the Inn, she had met all kinds of people both rich and poor. She believed one's luck at birth was not an indicator as to one's eventual worth. Hard work, integrity and kindness as well as their opposites could be found at all class levels.

A mixture of dreamer and pragmatist, she was well aware of the realities of Spanish society. Centuries of this class hierachy had changed little but she felt far removed from it at the Inn. Most of the realities played out in Madrid and other cosmopolitan cities. The Church, however, was a strong influence in all of the country, that was inescapable and Elena was no exception. Her belief in the protection of the Church, in particular the Virgin, played a central role in her life.

More than one young man had expressed interest in the shy, pretty girl and she received their attentions but with little interest. Like most girls her age, she secretly dreamed of her ideal suitor. Her dream man would be handsome and well dressed, not like most of the young men around her. He must be well- spoken, show beautiful manners and all with just a hint of mystery. The latter was a most important trait.

For as comfortable as she was in her present circumstance, she began to see her future and she was slightly troubled. The idea of spending her whole life in Albacete, doing the same thing, seeing the same people seemed boring.

"Maybe, someday, this man will come and show me the world. New places! New people."

Something of the sort would come about for the young woman but it not quite what she had envisioned when Fernando Sanchez came to town.

Fernando Sanchez had heard of Elena and had come to see if all he had heard was true. He discovered that her family was respectable and had some wealth. Not only had she developed the reputation as a fair, but savvy business, she was very attractive. All in all, she was just what he was looking for.

He lost no time in pressing his suit and followed protocol; presenting himself first to her parents. Stressing his impeccable family history and respect, he impressed the Don and Dona. He spoke mostly of his biological family in Gandia, not his adoptive parents and they were mentioned only as a stable source of income:the leather shop. He continued to explain that their daughter would be in fine hands and lack for nothing and purposely left the impression that he, Fernando, ran the leather business. And that, if accepted,

Elena would live well as she raised their future grandchildren. The Don seemed satisfied.

The first step accomplished, Fernando turned his energies to the daughter.

He had done his homework, enquiring about her likes and dislikes and showed up daily under her balcony window laden with flowers and sweets.

His determination was clear as he wooed the girl with gifts, words of admiration and longing. For her part, Elena was soon taken with his polished airs, manners and impeccable dress. And she had to admit: he was certainly handsome!

Slowly, she warmed to the persistent young man. As custom dictated, the couple were not to be left alone. Chaperones were ever present leaving no opportunities for any public displays of affection, or, God forbid, any "mischief" ! A prospective bride's honor was not to be tarnished. In time, he was invited to dinner and the marriage arranged.

After the wedding, Fernando returned to the Navarros with Elena. He had certainly achieved his goal:his wife could now assist his adoptive father in the shop and he would resume his pleasures. Mission accomplished!

Gradually realizing that she had been "a prize," her spirits fell. But she was a married woman now, and she was expected to obey her husband. Her desire for excitement and novelty would turn out, in reality, to have even more of the same drudgery but she would make the best of it.

Fernando's adoptive parents warmly welcomed her. And she liked the couple and admired them for accepting and raising her new husband. Their warmth reminded her of some of her own family and that helped with the transition to her new home.

Initially, she could not understand Fernando's distant attitude toward her and the couple but decided it was his difficulty adjusting to the marriage.

Perhaps his tendency to gruffly speak to her and the couple would change in time. Adding to her dismay was the old man and woman's seeming acceptance of his condescending attitude. Where was his respect?

He visited the marital bed quite frequently, so he must have found her desireable. She had shown him her devotion with hard work and compliance.

Puzzled, Elena was determined to make her new husband love her even more.

What she soon discovered was that love, for Fernando, had never been a factor in choosing her.

"The art of being wise is the art of knowing what to overlook."

William James

Chapter Five

It had been almost five months since the Civil War had been officially proclaimed. Most of Albacete's population had some idea of their country's political turmoil and everyone held a strong opinion as to which side, the Republican Red or Fascist White represented the "true' Spain. Most of these exchanges became heated in the communities bars and cafes but rarely led to any real violence. Sporadic fighting between the parties became increasingly common, but only in parts of the country as the two sides grouped, advanced or lost ground, then regrouped again. This pattern would continue for more than three years prolonging the outcome, as each side was fully convinced in their eventual triumph. But Franco's superior military might, fueled by the Church's power, would make the final call.

Located directly across from Albacete's rail station, Manolo's family inn was well positioned. There were several in the city, all providing food, drink and lodging for travelers. But the Sanchez Posada inn was special. It was the only large inn with direct access to the railway. This was a crucial site that enabled supplies, arms and freedom fighters easy access to major route in all directions.

Logistically, the site was perfect and roughly one hundred and seventy five miles from the capital; Madrid.

Built in the style of the time, it had several balconied bedrooms on the second floor complete with a open, box shaped courtyard below. The dining area, office and kitchen were located on the first floor as well as the private family and servants' quarters. Running such a large establishment demanded more than just the family's work so a cook, a handyman and a few servant girls were hired to help.

As a son of a middle class family, nine year old Manolo had some chores but beside those and attending school, he had much free time. His Tia Rosario lived with the family and it seemed her existence was centered around pampering her adored nephew. Whether hand feeding him his dinner or combing his shiny black hair, Tia's attention was constant. Manolo's two sisters complained about their brother's special treatment but not too seriously as they often joined in taking care of the boy. And for his part, the boy thought nothing of it.

A quiet and thoughtful boy, Manolo returned the affections to all of the females in his family. He would admit to no one, certainly not his friends, that he loved all the attention. All of this affection and care convinced him that women were worthy of respect, kindness and caring. It was obvious that his father didn't share his views.

"I don't understand why Papa is so rough and mean and rude to them. Abuelo isn't like that. I won't ever be like Papa!"

Sitting in the courtyard, surrounded by his play things, Manolo was too absorbed in his thoughts to notice several men enter. As he looked up, he saw that they all seemed to be speaking at once but more ominously, all carried rifles.

"Dios Mio! What's going on?"

This was Manolo's first encounter with the Lincoln Brigade. The decision had been made to quarter them at the Posada and it was that day that he began to understand that the war was going to change his world forever.

Suddenly, the Inn seemed to come alive all at once. Men and women were shouting for Papa and Mama and thankfully, Abuelo was visiting at that hour.

Drawn by the servants'shouts, his parents came rushing into the courtyard. As the boy stood behind them, the leader of the soldiers approached.

"I am ordered to inform you that we, the Lincoln Brigade, are to take possession of this property in service to Spain's Republic!You are honored to surrender the Inn in such service!"

The man spoke in a funny accent. In fact, Manolo could hear many strange languages as the Lincoln Brigade was a smaller unit of the international brigade.

Later he would learn that the speaker was Andre Marty, a Frenchman and leader of the Lincolns.

"You have one hour to clear the Inn of everyone. You may take a blanket, some clothes, but nothing else. Understand? NOTHING ELSE!"

At that point, Manolo's father found his voice. "But senor, it is winter! The coldest on record.. colder than Moscow! And our animals, our livelihood, food..." Marty's voice became ominous. "I repeat once only. Nothing else.You must understand this is an honor for you! Now go!"

Everyone scrambled to comply. This Marty fellow looked like he would not hesitate to use physical violence to make his point. Each of the servants and family members grabbed a blanket, a bit of bread and vacated the Inn. The servants could return to their familes but the Sanchez family had few options since they had just lost their home. Abuelo appeared in the courtyard.

"Come home with me, now. There's room and we can sort out this mess later."

Abuelo's arms were around Elena and the girls as Manolo slowly walked behind trying his best to avoid Papa's murderous look. Each carried one blanket and as much dignity as possible. They soon came to Abuelo's large house where Abuela, his grandmother was waiting. Seeing the ragged group, she burst into tears. All the adults began talking at once about the outrage and opinions so no one noticed when the boy slipped away. Somewhat confused, Manolo ran back to his home and as he entered the courtyard, he encountered a shocking scene:

Soldiers were tossing his toys, HIS toys, to an assembly of children below!He recognised a few but others were strangers. He could hear some of the men shouting in English and may have not understood the words but he certainly understood what was happening.

"OK, kids. Here ya go! Plenty for all! Everybody gets one!"

The men were laughing and seemed to be enjoying themselves as they were distributing his belongings to the children. Confused, hurt and freezing, he ran back to his grandfather's home. Abuelo, understanding the boy's pain, gently explained that the new Socialist

Republic meant that everyone was equal so even children must share their toys with those who had none.

Intellectually, the boy understood the concept, after all, he had proudly memorized the Communist anthem and his nine year old's immagination reveled in the excitement of a new Spain. He was proud to be a Spaniard and dreamed of a return to the days of Spain's glorious past; the 15th and 16th centuries of conquest, riches and world power. He was well aware that his father did not share the same ideas. Fernando was pro-German, therefore, pro-Franco, unlike Abuelo. Identifying with his grandfather came naturally and gave Manolo more than a little satisfaction that again, he was nothing like his father.

The emotional reality was a different story and it was just beginning to sink in. He had lost his home and his beloved possessions all in the same day! Mama and the girls were crying with Abuela and Papa's dark looks reminded him of his father's expectations to "act like a man." in other words:stand straight, proud and show no emotion.

"I won't cry...I won't! I'm a soldier too!" Manolo would not show any tears now. "I am a man, like Abuelo says. Just a short one in short pants!"

Chapter Six

As a boy, Manolo wanted to be just like his Abuelo. When Abuelo needed the aid of a cane to walk, the boy fashioned a stick into a crude cane to mimic his uneven gait. As school was open only sporadically because of the war, the boy spent much of his time with his grandfather. He would run errands or help with packages; anything for Abuelo. On special days he would accompany both his grandparents to the Cafe for a treat:his beloved churros and rich chocolate while the adults enjoyed their coffee. It was almost as good as going to church with Mama. Well, almost.

He loved escorting his mother to the neighborhood church and felt pride to be the "gentleman" and not Papa to be escorting "his lady." Every few days, Dona Elena and her eldest son made the mile walk to the church. Once inside, Manolo genuflected, kneeled, sat, kneeled again until the end of the service. But these rituals were superficial for the boy as his mind was on more important matters; when his friends would arranged the next soccer game or what was for dinner. He convinced himself that he was keeping up his end of his duties; his end of the bargain with God by coming to church.

After church, it was God's turn.

The walk home proved far more pleasurable. On the way was a cafe that sold candies and pasteries and Dona Elena was one of it's best customers.

Before returning home from their devotions, mother and son stopped for a treat; chocolates, churros, candies. God was very good, indeed!

Now, Abuelo kept a horse and buggy for business as well as for pleasure and he was very fond of his old horse for he had served his master well for many years. Reliable and gentle, the horse knew his master's commands and sensed his preference for a slow, gentle pace.

Manolo had different ideas. "This horse is terrible, Abuelo! Too slow! I bet he can really move if you let him. Give me a try, I'll make him go."

Ginez knew better. "Manolo, I told you that I will drive him. You're only nine years old, much too young. When you get older, then I'll think about it."

"Aw, Abuelo. All right. But I'm going to give him a name:Alma Muerta!"

Ginez doubled over in laughter. Alma Muerta meant "Dead Soul." He could always depend on his grandson to make him laugh! He soon found that Manolo could elicit other emotions as well.

Four months later, Ginez was hospitalized with a gallstone attack. The operation went smoothly and he was to be released from the hospital but there was a problem:no one was available to drive him home. His servant had left the horse and buggy at the hospital assuming one of the family would come and drive Ginez home. Alone, Manolo arrived at the hospital.

"But Abuelo! I can do it! Let me prove it! I'll do everything like you taught me and go real slow. Please give me the chance! It will be such an honor and besides, you get to go home sooner!"

Relunctantly the old man agreed. He was anxious to go home. He hated hospitals, they were for sick people and he was fine.

"Manolo, Only if you drive him slowly, very slowly. I want to get home in one piece!"

"I'll just take it slow, Abuelo!Just like you said. Old Alma Muerta won't go any faster anyway.. or will he?"

"Dios Mio!" Ginez yelled, hanging on for dear life as the horse and buggy took off like a shot. The horse looked confused at first, but quickly picked up the pace. Manolo was convinced that he was enjoying the ride as much as he. The boy gave the horse free reign knowing he would follow the same route to his home. Ginez's face turned ashen as the horse came to a sudden stop at the front door. Manolo grinned and turned to his grandfather.

"See? Home safe and sound and in record time, too! Boy, that was great! That horse is better than I thought. Now that I have the hang of it, want me to do some errands for you?"

"No, Manolo. Enough for one day." As his grandson helped him into the house, he muttered, "What I need now is a good stiff drink!"

A few months later, Gimez had another intestinal attack but this one proved more serious. Within a few months, Manolo had to say a final goodbye to his beloved Abuelo. At the cemetary, as the service was concluding, Manolo's tears began to flow. Seeing his son, Fernando responded.

"Stop crying. Be a man!"

Although only nine years old, his father's angry words stunned him into submission and he quickly composed himself. The feelings of abject grief, however, continued.

"You'll never have a quiet world till you knock the patriotism out of the Human Race."

George Bernard Shaw

Chapter Seven

The old man had been employed at the Posada for nearly three decades, long before it was handed over to Dona Elena. Her father had given him a job as a stable hand but quickly saw his potential and promoted him to Supply Manager.

He took the responsible position very seriously and performed it well. He genuinely liked and respected Don Ginez whom he found fair and just. Why, when he had married and started his own family, his employer had encouraged his own children to play with his!The Manager was especially fond of the Don's daughter Elena as she shared many of her father's traits and ideas. Both believed that hard, honest work was far more important and one's so called "pedigree" and father and daughter always treated him as a loyal and trusted friend, not just as an employee.

Her husband was a different matter. Fernando barked orders to him, demanding that chores be done on his demand. With his gruff and sarcastic tone, he implied that the employees were to be treated as such; mere employees.

Unsettled but loyal, the Manager continued to work hard and showed no negative emotions. He rationalized that Dona Elena and her father were his employers, not Fernando.

But the Manager's son felt differently. Since his school days, the old man had been concerned about his son. He proved quick to anger but worse, struck out at any person, animal or object that had the misfortune to be close at hand when the son's wrath exploded. No amount of training, education or punishment seemed to change this worrisome trait. The young man was bright and a hard worker but he had lost many jobs because of his temper. Unemployed, he was spending his time with like minded young men whose idea of a day well spent was to drink at the bars all the while bemoaning their fate. In their minds, anyone who was a "Francoista, " a White supporter was asking for trouble. Slights, real or imagined were blown out of proportion and inflated as each man vied for the gang's attention recounting personal tales of disrespect, abuse and dishonor.

The Manager's son often chided his father, "Papa, how do you stand it? That swine Sanchez treats you like a peasant and you just take it! In the new and glorious Spain, he will be shot or hanged as the enemy he is."

"My son, you are still young. So hot blooded! Just ignore Senor Sanchez like I do. I work for Don Ginez and Dona Elena. They have always been kind and respectful to us so don't let your temper rule you."

But the son's pent up frustration was too strong and needed an outlet; he wanted an outlet! His opportunity came a few days later when he overheard a conversation between two of his family members; his father and fifteen year old sister.

"Has he...touched you?" The Manager could barely get the words out.

"No, Papa, no...He just smiles at me sometimes. Sometimes winks but it makes me so uncomfortable! Please, Papa, ask him to stop!"

"I will speak to the Senor. I'm sure he means no harm."

The son had heard enough. This was too much. it was bad enough to see his father humiliated, but his sister? "It's a matter of family honor and I will have my honor restored!" He would say nothing about his eavesdropping to either one. "Let him talk...I will act."

All of the Inn's employees did their best to avoid Fernando. His mood seemed to be sullen or angry and dealing with Dona Elena was easier. She always asked about each one's health and family and made sure they had what they needed; whether food or medicine. Avoiding Fernando was fairly easy as he was rarely home anyway. His foolish pretense of being an 'elite" was a source of ridicule and disgust as most people were aware of his personal history. But Fernando still had some control over their livelihood.

They were all hopeful that soon, the tide would turn and a new Republican Spain would level the playing field once and for all. The people would rule and everyone would be judged on his own merit and not his ancestral bloodlines.

The Manager's son was also convinced that this new Spain was close at hand and prayed he would live long enough to benefit from it. But formost in his mind was the need to exact his revenge on Senor Fernando Sanchez.

"When that day comes, Sanchez will pay dearly for treating us so poorly. Papa can't see it now but he'll be glad when the day come. I will make him pay for this."

The Manager and his family were asked to stay on at the Posada once the Lincoln Brigade had commandeered it. It was felt by Marty that his troops needed to concentrate on battle readiness, not household tasks and the old man was grateful for the work and continued as if nothing had changed much. Change would come soon enough.

In Albacete, there was growing resentment towards any person with White political leanings; people such as Fernando. He no longer felt safe around the town as it semed to him that almost overnight, Albacete had turned "Red." He spent less and less time around town and more at his in-laws.

In the Posada, news came from the authorities that any "White" sympathizer was to be rounded up and detained. No one was safe. Here was the chance the Manager's son had been waiting for! Now the shoe was on the other foot.

The young man had no trouble assembling a group of men for his cause as many wanted revenge on the elitist bastards. Fernando Sanchez was a good start. The small group, armed with pistols and knives made their was toward their prey. Finally, revenge was at hand.

Don Ginez had heard the plans as well and secreted his daughter and her family to Alcala de Jucar, a small river town twenty miles away. He was not confident that his daughter and grandchildren would be spared by anyone seeking revenge and was well aware of his son-in-law's dangerous political position. Fernando had put the whole family in jeopardy and he must act...and now.

The family drove, in the dead of night, to the town where another family had been staying. Only two people had known of the plan; his wife and the Manager. They could be trusted to remain silent and profess ignorance of the family's whereabouts.

The Manager had the greatest admiration for Dona Elena and although he shared his son's dislike for her husband, he wished him no harm. But he was not sure that given the chance, his son would not harm the entire family. He fully realized that his son was out for blood and would take any opportunity to get revenge.

The clock's chimes could be heard in the nearly deserted Posada. The only person staying at the Inn was the trusted Manager, as someone needed to stay for safety. In these troubled times, an empty house was an open invitation for burglery; or worse.

The pounding at the front door startled the Manager. He was half awake as it very late. The only person that it could possibly be was Don Ginez.

"Probably forgot something." he thought, " But he has his key..."

The insistent pounding increased as he headed toward the door and as he opened it, he could not hide his astonishment. There, with several other men was his son. The group pushed their way inside.

"Where is he?Where is that...that bastard?" The Manager had never seen his son so agitated and he swallowed hard to find his voice.

"I...I don't know, son. No one's here. Don Ginez is out and I'm here to check the house."

"What kind of a fool do you take me for? Now, where are they ?" Enraged, he struck his father.

"I'm warning you, old man. Next time it's this!" His son cocked the pistol and pointed it at his father's head.

"This isn't really happening! my own son? You would shoot me? Your own father?" he suddenly felt a warm, wet flow down his trousers. In his terror, he had lost control of his bladder. The other men started to laugh but quickly stopped as the saw the look on the son's face.

"Shut up, you fools! We have business here."

"Son, son...please! Dona Elena, the children."

"None of your concern. Now, for the last time. And I'm warning you...Where did they go?"

Beaten and fearing for his own life, the Manager told his son what he wanted; the place where the family had fled to safety. As soon as they had obtained the information, they left. Alone, the old man began to cry.

"God forgive me! And God forgive my son!"

"Nobody, as long as he moves about the chaotic currents of Life is without trouble."

Carl Jung

Chapter Eight

The night flight to Alcala de Jucar took hours as it was difficult to navigate the dark dirt roads. Finally, Fernando found the designated place.

There had been little said during the trip as everyone was still in shock from the recent develpments. Exhausted and frightened, they had found safety at last.

Perhaps...

The inhabitants of the house were also in hiding; a family of husband, wife and two small children. Introductions were made and both families made feeble attempts at sleep.

The strong morning sun woke the boy and Manolo felt some confusion as he opened his eyes. Staring at him was another boy! As he jumped out of the make shift bed, he looked around. It took him a few seconds to clear his mind and recall last night's adventure but as the other boy was roughly the same age, the boys quickly forgot any earlier shyness and started chatting about their mutual interests.

In the dining room, the rest of the Sanchez family were discussing the situation with the other family. Manolo's sisters sat in the corner trying to make some sense out of it all and were glad to see their brother enter the room; it gave them a little distraction. The next few days were spent in fear and anxiety as each family did their best to peacfully co-exist.

Dona Elena and the other woman stayed mostly in the kitchen preparing simple meals and catching up on any news while the two men occupied the parlor immersed in political debate.

"Bah, these Communists will ruin the country! Can you imagine Spain run by peasants? By God, the Germans have the right ideas!Superior might and order by superior people!" Both men shared similiar ideas.

The men suddenly stopped talking as something had caught both their attentions. They both had a clear view to the mountain and ridge road from the parlor and what they saw was ominious. Parked on the ridge were two trucks and filled with men and they could see that all had rifles and one man had begun the descent down the ridge... straight towards the house.

The ancient Medieval town of Alcala de Jucar had a river that ran through the center. The older sections, dotted by shops and homes, had been built directly into the side of the limestone mountain and each dwelling had been purposely carved into the mountain so that at first glance, one could only see the mountain and a lone road winding down to the valley below; a very clever disquise and defense to protect against any potential threat or foe. The two families were hiding in a house at the bottom of the ridge, and had the situation not been so dire, they may have been able to appreciate the spectacular view up the mountain.

As it was, the scene was unfolding before the women as well.

"Oh my God. Children, quickly. Manolo. Where is Manolo?"

The two boys were sauntering around the house after playing around the backyard. As they entered they house, they froze. Everyone was huddled together as if expecting the worse. Someone started pounding on the door.

"Open this door in the name of the glorious Republic."

Trapped, the men glanced at each other. The pounding and shouting continued but by now, resignation had set in and the door was opened.

"You! Come with me!" Armed with a rifle and pistol, the soldier was pointing at the other man, not Fernando. Perplexed, the two men stared at each other.

"You are ordered to come with me. At once!"

"And my family?"

"Only you. They stay. But I warn you! If you resist, we will all come down here and shoot you all."

Trembling, the man hugged his wife and children. As he held them, he assured them that all would be well. He would go and straighten it all out. This was all just a big mistake, a terrible misunderstanding. He then left with the soldier to make the trek back up the ridge. Everyone watched them go.

A few minutes passed as the man seemed to be speaking to someone in command and he was gesturing with both hands spread as if in supplication. But at a signal, several armed men jumped out of the trucks and began firing on the hapless and defenseless man.

Manolo covered his ears at the deafening sounds and the women were screaming at the unfolding horror. The machine guns had cut his body into pieces and the power was so great that it appeared the man's body was being controlled by some unseen puppeteer. Sickened but mesmerized, Manolo continued to watch until he remembered his mother. She had fainted as soon as she saw the man fall.

As suddenly as they had appeared, the death squad disappeared. It seemed a strange twist of fate that Fernando had not been their target as he had believed.

The villagers began to slowly come out of their homes once the trucks left as this sort of madness was happening everywhere; both sides were engaged in the terror. The only semblence of safety was to stay in your home. Some people retrieved the man's body as others tried to comfort the grieving widow and her children. It was eerily quiet as people milled around in shock.

Elena gathered her children around her and turned to her husband, "They know we are here and they'll come for us next..."

The days passed without incident as the Sanchez family wavered between staying put or waiting for news from Don Ginez. But if they left, where would they go? Who could they trust?

As they were discussing their next move, they spied a speeding car winding down the road toward the valley and making straight for them! Elena shouted for the children to get back into the house but Fernando stayed in the yard expecting the worse. Whoever was at the wheel was driving as if the Devil himself were chasing him! He decided to stand outside and face his enemies, whoever they may be. But as the automobile came closer, Fernando's bravado began to waver.

At that moment, the car screeched to a halt directly in front of him. His astonishment grew as he recognized his brother-in-law! How was this possible?

He lived in Alicante, another province many kilometers away so how had he known?Unlike Fernando, Elena's brother was pro-Red and was working as a chauffeur for the Alicante provincial goverment. In addition, he was well respected and liked by the Republican governor of the province.

"Fernando! Where are Elena and the children?Quickly, there's no time to lose! "he shouted as he waved a document. Fernando cautiously approached his brother-in-law.

"But how?How did you know where we were?" asked Fernando.

"I'll tell you once we get the family in the car. There's not much time Get everyone in! Pronto! I have all the documents for safe passage back to Albacete, now GO!"

Upon seeing her brother, Elena hustled the children out to the waiting car.

She had gathered their meager belongings since the flight from Albacete happened so quickly that all they really had were the clothes on their backs, a small amount of money and some food.

The car roared off as swiftly as it had arrived. Tio could hardly get a word in edgewise between Fernando's questions and Elena's sobs. Even his nephew Manolo was bombarding him with questions.

"Tio, Tio...How did you know where we went? Did Abuelo tell you? Huh, Tio?"

"Enough Manolo," chided his mother." Let Tio talk!"

The boy finally quieted and listened to the adult conversation to learn of the events. After the family had fled Albacete, Manolo's grandfather had made a telephone call to his son in Alicante. Knowing he worked for the Alicante government as a special chauffeur and ambulance driver and was well respected as a loyal Republican, perhaps he could explain the peril his family was in to his superiors and secure the proper documents to ensure their safety.

And so he did.

It had taken several hours but the documents were signed and by the highest office; the governor of Alicante. Any Republican soldier would certainly honor them as it mentioned each family member by name and to ensure it's validity, they were stamped with the governor's own seal.

The documents were passed around as each marveled at the idea that a simple proclamation was their ticket out of Hell, for that is how they had come to think of the last few day:pure Hell. But they were becoming more comfortable and excited as the car moved towards the next town.

"Dios Mio." Elena quickly made the "sign of the cross" and cupped her hands over her daughters' eyes, but it was too late. What was before them was not only terrifying but grotesque.

The car slowed as the scene unfolded. Dead bodies of men and a few women and children could be seen on the side of the road. They appeared to have been shot or knifed and the only living souls around seemed to be those survivors trying to gather the remains for burial. Except for the moaning and wails of the living, the air was silent.

"Mama, Papa. Who did this?" Manolo stopped before his parents could shush him. He felt sick to his stomach as the same scene was unfolding as they drove further.

"Don't look at that!Look straight ahead!" barked his Tio. Manolo couldn't hear the hushed conversation between his father and uncle but had little trouble obeying. If he let his natural curiosity prevail, his stomach would surely revolt. Glancing at his pale and trembling sisters, he remained quiet.

The car drove on for a few more kilometers only to arrive at a roadblock.

Several trucks, similiar to the ones that had stopped at Alcala de Jucar's ridge had blocked the road. Everyone's fear level rose. This couldn't be happening again?The family was shocked to see a few women with rifles in the group and they were all pointing at the family!

"Out of the car, now!" shouted a soldier." Up against that house!.. that wall!" Everyone did as they were directed. Holding the documents, Tio explained that they all had official safe passage.

"Means nothing to me!" replied a soldier." See the Captain overthere! The rest of you, all of you! Stand there against that house... against that wall!"

Elena pleaded," But my children!"

"Shut up, woman!"

The family had no choice so they did as they were told.

The small cadre of armed soldiers raised their guns, pointing at the entire family. Fernando held his daughters as Elena shielded Manolo behind her skirts.

"This can't be happening!" she cried but she refused to close her eyes. She stared straight into the man's eyes and wanted him to remember the family's killer. She wanted him to always remember her look. A soldier ordered the squad to ready their arms and on his command, shoot...until dead. The boy could hear the multiple clicks of the cocked rifles and began to pray as he asked God to forgive him for everything and make a place for them all in Heaven. He hoped it was enough.

Tio had spoken to the group's leader and insisted they were making a terrible mistake. The leader of the soldiers took his time as he read the papers, suspicious of a forgery but when he finally saw the actual signature and seal, he called to the squad.

"Stop! Lower your arms and let them go! They have clearance."

Tio and the man began to walk toward the house but the rifles remained in place. The tension did not lessen until the order was repeated.

"Are you deaf?I ordered you to lower your arms and NOW! Let them pass."

It was obvious to all that the soldiers were not happy at losing the opportunity to rid the country of five more suspected Fascists. Emotions were clearly overiding any need to examine the reality or truth.

Everyone shared the same unspoken thoughts; if these people wanted to harm them, who else? Paranoia was settling in on the Sanchez family as it was on most of the families in Spain. And this anxiety would not lift for another forty years until 1975, the year of Franco's death.

Outside the car window, the scenes remained nightmarish. The only way to escape the horrific scenes was to keep one's eyes shut as Elena had instructed. The girls gladly complied but Manolo's curiosity got the better of him. He was repelled yet fascinated at seeing all these dead people and the men who had been responsible for their deaths. One scene, in particular became imprinted on his mind. As the passed, a man, obviously dead, was slumped by the side of the road, covered in olives. Perhaps an olive merchant?

Waves of nausea overtook the boy and he knew he would never, ever, eat another olive as long as he lived.

They all appeared to be ordinary villagers, victims and executioner alike.

The grave diggers could barely keep up with the demand for as each body was laid to rest in a hole, more shots rang out signaling more executions.

Manolo didn't dare ask any more of the multiple questions he had for a glance at the somber faces on the adults warned him to remain silent. There would be time for questions once they reached Albacete and relative safety. For now, he simply stared at the ongoing violence that was playing out along side of the road.

"The heart has it's reasons which Reason knows nothing of."
Blaise Pascal

Chapter Nine

The Socialist had stayed in control of Albacete for several months after the escape to Alcala de Jucar. The "Reds," in an attempt to salvage some of Albacete's young, developed a policy of rescue. Bolshevic Russia would accept Spain's children for the duration of the war, reportedly with the stated idea of returning them once peace was secured. They offered families a plan for getting their children safely to Russia but were vague with any plans for return.

Following their orders would be in the interest of their children and the glory of the Communist movement abroad. Why, compliance would be a courageous act of patriotism to the "Cause" ! In spite of misgivings, many families did comply as it seemed at least, a guarantee for the children's safety. Manolo's family was not one of them.

Both Elena and Fernando were not convinced of the plan. It didn't seem to have any solid base and they were suspicious of the fact that especially boys between the ages of six and twelve were being targeted. Elena especially, was not about to send her Manolo to a foreign country, and alone! No, she would never do so. They had to think of something.

Luckily, the men tasked with collecting the children were not from Albacete. They were handpicked Communists who spoke Russian and Spanish.

They had a list of families within the target age group and were assigned to go from house to house to get them. One of the Sanchez servants overheard the gossip that their street was next.

Loyal friends and employees were stationed in the neigborhood so as to give ample warning to the family. The day came when one spotted the men. It was hard to miss them since they all wore particular jackets and addressed everyone and each other as comrade; not the usual senor, senora, or senorita.

Manolo's two sisters went to the kitchen to help the cook as their mother gathered all of Manolo's belongings and hid them in a large covered basket. She then instructed him to stay under the bed. She told him, in no uncertain terms, to stay there until she came for him; no one else. Frightened at the prospect of being taken from his family, especially from Mama, he did exactly as instructed. He calmed himself by the memory of the graveyard executions and told himself this was just another example of his bravery.

There was a sudden knock on the courtyard door. Fernando walked over and opened it. There stood two men, waving papers.

"Comrade, we have papers here to take your son to safety... to Mother Russia. We have come for him," spoke one man.

"There must be some mistake! I have no son! I mean," he stuttered, "There is the baby, as you can see and my daughters are here. But they are six and fifteen, surely you don't mean them?" Fernando tried his best to look innocent and confused and prayed he was convincing.

"No comrade, we only have room for the boy. Our papers state that you have a son around the age of ten living here," the man replied." We will look for ourselves, if you don't object."

Knowing any thing but total compliance might alert them of his deceit, Fernando stepped aside and invited them in. He maintained his smile but was troubled at the men's faces.

They seemed to be smirking and it reminded him of how a cat's facelooked just before it pounced on it's prey. He started sweating.

Fernando led the men into the kitchen where he pointed to his daughters.

Room by room, the men searched for the missing boy, sure of finding him. They finally came to Dona Elena's bedroom where she sat quietly mending a shirt. Next to her was a cradle containing a peacefully sleeping baby Jaime.

"Fernando! Who are our guests?" she asked softly.

"These men are from the Save Spain's Socialist Children's Project and they seem to think we have an older son!"

"Oh? No...other than our baby here, we have no other.... two girls, yes, but another son? No...maybe God will bless us with another in the future. I think, gentlemen, that someone gave you a wrong list. It's all so confusing sometimes, isn't it?" She gave the men her sweetest smile.

Fernando looked at his wife with some admiration. She spoke convincingly and without hesitation and he hoped her act convinced the men. Glancing at the list, then at each other, the men left the room muttering, " Damn these Spaniards! They just can't organize anything!"

Making sure the men had left, Elena retrieved the boy and instructed one of the servants, the cook, to stay with Manolo in the room, just in case. It would be disasterous for the family if their little ruse had failed. She had felt badly for one of her neighbors who had tried a similar plan. The Communists who had been sent to collect the boy had been met with similiar protests. Somehow, they became suspicious of the family's denial. They left, waited a few moments around the corner, then returned to find the hidden boy. Amid tears and struggle, the boy was put on a waiting truck and sent to Russia never to return.

Elena was taking no chances with her son.

Their fears were well founded. Those children did not leave Russia for many years, if at all. As adults, in the 1960s, they were brought back to Spain. As many had married and had families of their own and having dim memories of their earlier life in Spain, most considered themselves Russian. They refused Spain's offer of repatriation and chose to return to their home:Russia. For many families, this turn of events was heartbreaking.

Less than a decade later, during WW2, the British government adopted a similiar plan. As the city of London was targeted by German bombers, the goverment sent thousands of the city's children to the relative safety of the English countryside to wait out the war. Unlike Spain, it had a solid plan for their return, so few London families even hesitated to comply. Years later, this very subject would become the backdrop of a series of best selling novels by the British author, C. S Lewis in his series: The Chronicals of Narnia.

Chapter Ten

Although the family was eventually allowed to return to the Posada, like all of Albacete's residents, they remained in their misery. Food shortages were extreme and women and children waited for hours in bread lines. Sometimes the food ran out resulting in angry mobs fighting each other. It was worse for the people who had supported another political view as they were simply thrown out of the line. They had to endure shame and ridicule along with hunger. All but the very well connected suffered tremendously.

Constant hunger was the norm for most families and the Sanchezs were no exception. Rationing was strictly enforced so Manolo was often sent with his sisters to stand in the long food lines. Curiosity and pre-adolescent bravado often got the better of him. As he watched the older boys cut into the lines or stole an item, he thought he was equal to the task. But he only was beaten back by the local Militia. He didn't give up. however and soon found ways to distract the authorities as he grabbed some bread or a handful of potatoes. His mother's delight at the purloined items were worth it.

Unknown to his parents, at times Manolo found himsef so starved that he resorted to rummaging through the pig troughs for any edible scraps of food; his empty stomach over ruling any sense of disgust or sense of danger as anyone caught taking food from farm animals was whipped, or worse. All animals were needed for the war effort.

Daily life had slowed to a crawl as families spent most of their time trying to find enough food and surviving, in general. With the help of Don Ginez, the family managed a meager existence but some families were not so fortunate and people died of starvation.

Years of any civil war takes a terrible toll on it's people and a depression hovered over the city. Shops, bars and restaurants were rarely opened for business with little merchandise or food. Families mostly stayed at home believing it the safest place should any skirmishes break out. Schools were open intermittently when fighting or bombings allowed.

Albacete's schools were under Communist control during this time. The emphasis was, of course, on their political and social ideals. As a powerful propaganda tool for inspiration of the new Left, school children were shown a Russian revolutionary newsreel made many years earlier.

During the nineteen twenties, Russia was undergoing her own revolution.

Peasant uprisings led by the left leaning Bolshevics overthrew the Russian Czar, executed him and his entire family in addition to his many aristocratic supporters.

A military group, the Marines of Kronstadt had been engaged in a battle with those loyal to the Czar but were soon defeated. As captured on newsreel, these sailors were rounded up, bound hands and feet and with a rope around their necks weighted with a large stone, thrown off a cliff into the sea and to their deaths. To the one, these men met their fates standing proud and without any struggle.

News footage of this event and the actual murders were shown repeatedly to the impressionable youths and they were challenged by school authorities to meet their destiny as valiantly as had the Marines. Ideals of bravery, sacrifice and honor were powerful, especially for any schoolboy and the authorities knew few would be immune to the challenge. Manolo was completely enthralled with the story and told it to anyone would would listen. In his young mind, he wanted to be every bit as brave as those Marines and looked for chances to prove it.

"Sometimes a cigar is just a cigar"
Sigmund Freud

Chapter Eleven

For the next several months, life for the Sanchez family focused on the basics and everything, except suffering was in constant short supply.

Without realizing it, Manolo had an early intoduction to peacetime. Hungry and bored, the boy wandered alone down the road along side the railroad tracks.

He often did so when he was preoccupied with his own thoughts and felt a need for solitude. Lost in his imagination, he had walked for several miles before he realized it and as he looked around, he could see no other living being, man or animal. He was totally alone.

"I better get back...it's really late and Papa will be upset with me again for holding up dinner, if you can even call it that. More lentils! And there's never enough!." Just as he turned to retrace his steps, he heard a distant sound "Sounds like a truck or motorcycle' thought the boy.

"I'll just walk a little slower and see who it is."

The sound grew louder and Manolo realized it was the distinctive roar of a motorcycle. But as the machine came closer, Manolo became fearful. There were two flags; one on each handlebar, and they were Italian! Aligned with Franco! And if that wasn't bad enough, he saw the man was in uniform with a rifle slung over his shoulder. One of Italy's Mussolini's troops!

"Dios Mios, It's the enemy.. And no place to hide!" He was all alone as he faced this danger and he could see no one within shouting distance. He was utterly at the soldier's mercy. Anxiety paralyzed him and he stood still as he thought, "If he talks to me, I'll pretend I don't understand...no comprendo...and maybe, if the Virgin is with me, he'll just keep going."

"Boy! Hey. You there! Boy!" called the Italian soldier. Christ, this kid looks half starved and frightened, thought the man. Thank God this war is over and I can soon leave this Godforsaken country. I'm sick to death of looking at hungry kids.

"For Chrissakes, kid, I'm not gonna hurt you. The war is over! You hear me?Over! Now, what do you want?" The soldier knew that although different languages, both Spanish and Italian had their roots in Latin so many words and phrases were similar. This kid must be scared to death, or deaf, or worse; dumb! Just my luck! I try to help some kid and he's retarded.

Looking at the soldier's backpack, Manolo spied a long loaf of bread; a baquette. In spite of trying to show no interest, he found himself salivating at the sight of a loaf of bread. He hadn't had anthing to eat since yesterday and knew dinner would be another plate of lentils. Lentils were the only food that seemed to be in great supply but the beans were keeping them alive. Wouldn't Mama love that pan, that bread. Eyeing the boy, the soldier smiled and pointed to his bag. "This what you want, kid?"

"Si.... pan," he replied slowly.

"Come on kid, here's the bread. Now, how would you like a ride home on my bike?" He motioned to Manolo to get on behind him.

Manolo practically shouted "Si! Por favor...Si!" at the offer.

"Well I guess the kid ain't dumb after all." The Italian helped secure him on on the back and off they roared. Manolo couldn't believe his luck and silently said a prayer of thanks to the Virgin Mary.

As they cruised close to the Posada, he saw his friends standing on the side of the road with their mouths wide open in disbelief.

"Manolo.Hey, it's Manolo." He, like all of his friends, had dreamed of someday riding on a motorcycle but not one of them had actually done so.

All transportation was consigned for military or business use only. Operating any vehicle for pleasure was strictly forbidden as the military needed the gasoline.

Manolo shouted to his friends standing outside. The combination of the motorcycle and excited, shouting children proved deafening for the soldier.

"Well, at least the kid's not a moron, that's for sure!" And for just this moment in his young life, Manolo forgot the suffering and hardship that seemed a permanent part of his life. Like any ten year old boy in his position, he felt on top of the world! Like anything, just anything was possible now that the war had ended.

"Madness need not be all breakdown. It may also be breakthrough. It is potential liberation and renewal as well as enslavement and existential death."

R. D. Laing

Chapter Twelve

For a time after the war, the sound of distant gunfire became a daily event and continued to elicit fear and anxiety. In the aftermath of a civil war, no one could be certain of who was killing whom.

"Mama!But who is shooting? Do we know them? Will they come for us, Mama?"

"Hush, Manolo," soothed Elena. "Don't listen. And don't worry...It doesn't concern us...we are safe."

Manolo wasn't so convinced but didn't want to contradict his mother.

Maybe she really didn't know what was happening and he wanted to protect her.

He had listened to the men's hushed conversations and had learned that the shooters; Franco's men, were routing out any remaining "Reds" that were perceived as threats.

His mother was not aware, no one was that Manolo sneaked out of the house and ran to the cemetary. Just before sunrise, he would climb upon one of the sloped rooftops to be able to peer over the ridge at the cemetary below.

This position allowed an expansive view but without the risk of detection. The scenes unfolding before him were as mesmorizing as repugnant but his curiosity compelled him to return for several mornings; until his mother found out about his wanderings. He could make out the people who were being lined up against one of the cemetary walls. They were mostly men, but occasionally a few women were among the group. And as bizarre as it may seem, a priest was present awaiting any condemned person's confession before he or she met death!No one took him up on the offer and instead, boldly sang the Socialist anthem. The firing squad lost little time in the executions and once the victims were pronounced dead, the bodies were left for the family's burial preparations.

These events jogged one of his early memories of an incident that had occurred in the early days of the Civil War while the family still resided at La Posada. Manolo had been at the cemetary to witness an extraordinary event.

In the same cemetary, four brothers of a local family had been shot as traitors, by the Red millitia.. A large crowd of Red sympathizers had gathered to witness the executions, as well as the unfortunate men's two sisters. Helpless, the sisters could only watch as their brothers were executed. In the bloody aftermath, the sisters washed the bodies and continued with the preparations for burial but as they were finishing and attempting to place a simple white cross on each brother's casket, they were interrupted by loud, threatening insults and other verbal abuse from the crowd. One of the sisters pulled out a pistol, aimed it at the crowd and cried, "I will shoot anyone, anyone who tries to touch those crosses or stop us! "

Eventually the crowd left the women, unmolested to complete their gruesome task.

“Man lives off Reason but survives off Dreams.”
Miguel Unamuno

Chapter Thirteen

Franco's Whites finally prevailed and the Civil War officially ended on April 1, 1939. Coincidently, April Fool's Day.

Unofficially, however, violence continued for several more months. The new prevailing Goverment sanctioned dozens of political executions, that was expected as the usual "cleansing" after most civil wars. But many more "revenge killings" kept people, especially those who had supported the Reds, in constant states of paranoia and anxiety.

After four years of Communist control, schools finally reorganized and Franco's Whites took them over. It was vital to educate Spain's children to the new political reality. A new conservative agenda and curriculum was in place with an emphasis on strict codes of compliance and duties to the new Fascist Spain and Church.

Under Communist control, religion and anything related was banned.

Those priests and nuns who had refused to go underground were expelled, tortured or killed and churches were closed in Albacete. Most would not open until the war's end.

Under Franco's dictatorship, the Roman Catholic Church, stronger than ever, sent Jesuit priests to Albacete's schools for a "spiritual exercise" (spiritual cleansing) or indoctrinations for those who had foolishly strayed from the Right Path:the Church's path. Schoolchildren were required to pledge allegience to the Church and new glorious leader and God's clearly chosen: General Francisco Franco. Any reference to Socialism or, God forbid Communism, whether books, songs or conversation was strictly forbidden and any infractions of these new laws from children or adults were met with harsh discipline. The New Order was especially hard on children. Their parents were old enough to remember the Church's power and it's centrality to everyday life but for nearly four years, most of Albacete's youngsters had lived their lives with little knowledge or contact with organized religion. They were woefully ignorant of expectations and more importantly, the Church's pervasive power.

"But Papa, I can go myself! I'm twelve now, almost a man!" protested Manolo as his father practically dragged him to the school.

"Ahhhh, but now you will be educated properly. And with some dicipline! You have become like a wild burro; wild and stubborn! And I want to make sure you get tamed!"

The hiatus from formal schooling had allowed some of the children to "run wild" and local neighborhood "gangs" were formed claiming imagined turf; mostly in imitation of the struggles around them. Most of the skirmishes involved pushing and shoving, but occasionally someone was actually hurt. Proudly, Manolo displayed the deep scar on his left forhead left by a stone hurled by a slingshot. The head wound had penetrated the cranium and become infected but the boy had been extremely lucky that no brain damage had occurred. Any comments about the dent in his forehead was often met with a boast, " Well, I guess I'm much stronger than Hercules! Maybe even Ulyssis!" .

Entering the school, Fernando sought out the Headmaster, Don Carlos. Short and rotund, he was slightly stooped and softspoken.

"Buenas Dias, Senor Sanchez! And what have we here? "

"What" is correct, Don Carlos. My son has lost his way and needs discipline, much dicipline and I don't care how you have to give it to him. He's in your hands now." With a look of disgust, Fernando glared at his son and walked home. Manolo suddenly felt cold. " I have a really bad feeling about this."

Looking at the Headmaster, he suddenly became frightened. He didn't like the the looks of the strange looking man. His enormous nose was hooked, his smile seemed permanently fixed, and his insipid manners hid something; of that the boy was certain. All in all, he looked like one of those birds of prey; like a vulture!He desperately wanted to go home but knew that wasn't an option.

"Dios Mios.This isn't going to be good but I must be brave and deal with whatever comes. I have to make Papa proud." he mused.

He quickly discovered his initial impression of the Headmaster was correct. Don Carlos seemed to spend his day visiting classrooms and meting out corporal punishment for the slightest perceived infraction. He was rarely seen without his black ruler as his favorite method of "dicipline" involved the palms of the hand.

"Manuel Sanchez! Stand up and follow me." Anytime one of the students heard his name uttered by the Headmaster, he froze in terror.

Manolo groaned and knew what was coming. Trying to explain that he was laughing at a friend's joke or that he had lost his pencil was useless, as all the children had learned; Don Carlos wasn't interested in any excuse.

The "Dicipline" was administered behind the closed doors of the Headmaster's office, partly to ensure privacy but mostly to create fear.

It was far more effective for the other school children to hear the screams and wails from the closed door than to witness it.

"Put your hands out. Palms up. Now let's see if this "spiritual cleansing" will bring you humbly back to self control!" At that moment, Don Carlos beat the boy's palms until they started to welt and bleed.

As many times as he and the other boys endured Don Carlos "discipline" they never seemed to remember the excruciating pain. Manolo knew the man was waiting for him to cry and beg forgiveness but he would not flinch.

Crying out would ensure more of the treatment and not submitting to this indignity was not an option as the consequences were too risky. No one, at least that he was aware of, dared challenge the authority of the Headmaster. The boy was brave but not without fear. He could withstand much of this Life's troubles but he wasn't about to condemn his very soul in the next. Sadly, he thought, "And to think that Papa believes I need so much dicipline. But why?"

Understanding that children were vunerable and easily manipulated, these educators set about changing their alliegences. Convincing young minds with the threat of dishonor, the lure of power and playing with their emotions proved rather easy. And even Manolo with his natural inquisitiveness and distrust of authority settled into the New Reality. It did take a little longer for him to accept the new doctrines but months of corporeal punishment, whippings in particular, eventually convinced him to change his loyalties.

Sadly, adults were not much different. Experience had taught most of them to remain quiet and keep any opinions to themselves. It was just too dangerous to publically discuss any dissenting ideas. A few intrepid souls, however, risked deportation or jail as they continued to question the authorities.

But not all of the educators were harsh. Some, like Don Jose were gentle and devoted to the students.

"Don Jose," smiled the Headmaster, " I know you believe in your heart that you are doing your best to teach these boys. But is it enough?I think you are much too soft. They need dicipline! After all, they've lived without our righteous guidance for years and it shows in their insolence and disrespect. They need to learn to show more respect but mostly, they need to obey!"

"Don Carlos, they're only boys! And mostly good boys! Their lives have been chaotic! Their families are suffering...not enough food, supplies and some have lost their fathers in the war. I think they need more guidance and... and understanding...por favor... please." Don Carlos was beginning to stutter.

The Headmaster cut him off "Understanding? Guidance? Humph...a bunch of unruly animals, that's what they are!And I intend to dicipline them into worthy men of the new Spain! "Buena Dias, Don Jose!" The Headmaster had clearly ended the conversation.

Back in his classroom, Don Jose" began to organize tomorrow's lessons. He's too harsh, too strict but he's my superior. I'd better not challenge him too much. I'll just keep my views to myself and help these boys make the transition as best I can."

Having survived the earlier private school, Manolo enrolled in The Institute to continue his education. The educators here stimulated his imagination and nurtured his intellectual curiosity. One such person was Dona Mercedes, the history professor. Seeing the boy's promise and particular interest in Ancient History, she spent extra time with him exploring the subject. Learning about the Roman sagas, Hannibal's exploits and the Cartheginians thrilled Manolo and under her tutelage, he flourished.

Studies aside, Manolo discovered a talent for soccer. He had always kicked a soccer ball around as soon as he could walk. Why, all the boys did. But he found he could play well in the Institute's organized team. Between his studies and soccer, he had little time for much else.

His relationship with his father did not appreciably change and he sadly accepted that his Papa just wasn't interested in him. This belief was made stronger when, unlike the other parents, Fernando did not attend any of his son's games. Eventually, Manolo no longer looked for him.

At the end of a particularly important match, one in which Manolo had scored the winning goal, his coach motioned to him and pointed, " Manolo, isn't that your father over there?There, behind that tree?" The coach knew all the boys and their families and Fernando was the only parent who had shown no interest in his son's performance.

Peering in the direction, he could just make out his father's hat and cane.

"I'm not sure, " he stammered, " Looks like him, but..." At that moment, the figure quickly disappeared.

"I'm sure it was, Manolo. And he was here for the entire game! He'll be really proud of you today! You played very well.Great job!"

Manolo was embarrassed but pleased at the coach's compliments. His hopes began to rise. Maybe Papa will say something at dinner! But nothing was said. Fernando just continued to eat and made no comments.

In this new cultural reality, the young teenager's allegiences changed from Communist Social Ideas to Franco's Social Control. The Falangistas were formed and patterned after Mussolini's Italy. Italy, as well as Germany was well aware of the emotional energy and maleability of youth. Organizing young men and boys into quasi-military groups proved to be a brilliant solution to a country rife with poverty, unemployment and with no real direction. Now, as one of them, Manolo proudly wore the signature "Blue Shirt" and could frequently be heard singing or humming the Falangista anthem "Cara al Sol."

Replete with a new found sense of importance, these youthful Franco loyalists embraced their new found sense of power and purpose, often to the point of intimidation. Sometimes, Manolo found himself the object of some bully's rage but returned blow for blow. After all, he was no coward, he was a Falangista rebuilding Spain... and a Castilian.

"Give all to love, obey the heart"
Ralph Waldo Emerson

Chapter Fourteen

Abuelo's death was difficult, as he felt closer to him than his own father.

But it was within the normal scheme of things that old people passed on so the pain soon lessened. Another family death, however, was a horrible shock.

Paloma, seven years older had been his oldest sister. She was trained in business and had a good local job. Still living at home, as was the custom until her upcoming marriage, her engagement to a fellow student was a source of pleasure for both families. Her carefree, pleasant manner won her many friends and admirers. Why, even her teasing of her little brother remained good natured as she really made no secret of adoring the "brat" .

As custom dictated, the family engaged a professional photographer for a formal portrait and Elena was especially pleased that they had secured an appointment with the famous Belda. Getting the entire family together, Mama, Papa, the girls, Manolo and seven year old Jaime was no small feat. Given this rare family outing, Elena scheduled her daughter's prenuptual medical exam immediately after the photograpy session. Paloma had not been feeling well lately but it was probably just pre-wedding jitters so the two women continued on to Dr. Venancio alone following the photography session, leaving the rest of the family to return home.

Dr Venancio formed a complete checkup, including X-rays and after he reviewed his findings, he asked both women to sit down.

"Senora, you must take her home immediately. And put her on strict bedrest."

The confused women looked at each other in alarm." But Doctor, I feel well!Just tired but I'm planning my wedding and there's so much to do!" Paloma replied. Her mother chimed in" See, I warned you about doing so much.I'll take over all the planning. I told you it was making you sick!"

Turning to Paloma, he gently picked up her hands and held them.

"My dear, I'm afraid it's more serious than fatigue...You are very ill,..... you have contracted tuberculosis and it's unfortunately advanced to both of your lungs."

Stunned, Elena started to rapidly speak, " Ok...Ok.... let me think. There's a sanatorium not too far from here. She'll just have to recouperate from there. We'll postpone the wedding. It will be fine.... I'll...."

"No!Senora, you don't understand. I'm sorry, there's no easy way to say this. Your daughter is dying.If she goes to the sanatorium, she'll just die there and alone. I recommend you take her home and put her on immediate bedrest. At least she'll be with loved ones."

The kindly doctor further explained that Paloma had contracted a virilant form of tuberculosis; sometimes known as "consumption." The lung disease was common around the country as evidenced by Spain's increased sanatorium hospitals. Built especially for isolation and treatment of this particular disease, there were scores continually being constructed.

Sometimes the treatments worked and after several months of isolation, the individual could reclaim his or her life. More often, however, it failed and death was the inevitable outcome.

"Ok...Ok...We'll put her in the hospital. We'll postpone the wedding until she's well. It will all work out, and I'll..."

"Mama! Stop talking. Listen to Dr. Venancio! He's trying to talk!" Paloma could see the troubled look on the doctor's face. She knew it was serious, deadly serious.

"Dona Elena, Paloma, I'm sorry. Again, There's no easy way to say this. It's beyond the sanatorium now. If Paloma goes to the hospital, she'll be on bedrest and some medications but more importantly, she'll be alone when her time comes. I can make her comfortable at home and she'll have her family around."

Slumping in the chair, the girl put her hands to her face and quietly wept.

Her mother straightened up and gravely asked, " How long Doctor?"

"A few months. I'm so sorry."

Neither Elena or her daughter could fully digest the news and walked home in a daze. All this excitement for the upcoming wedding and now it wouldn't happen? Dead in a few months?

As they entered the Posada, only Manolo and a few servants were home.

Fernando was at his usual place, the Cafe, engaged in a competative game of Dominos.

"Dios mio! Where is God now? "yelled Manolo when he heard the news. "It's not fair! Paloma has always been so good, so full of life! Why is this happening?"

Seeing his mother and sisters weeping, he stormed out of the house in a rage. He would return a while later when he could get his emotions under control.

He must not let them see his tears. They needed someone to lean on; a man and somehow he suspected his father would fail them, once again.

At seventeen, Manolo was the picture of health. He fit the classic' tall, dark, and handsome"description. Playing soccer or basketball for his high school teams, he could hear the girls giggle and call him "Ulyssus" . His teamates teased him mercilessly about it but he just ignored them as if the girl's admiration was all inconsequential. He may have ignored them, but secretly was pleased at the attention. Being" worshipped from afar" tapped into his idea of himself: a heroic figure, pure of heart and soul.. Like the mythical figures of old. But this self image also hid his inherent shyness and introverted personality.

Several times, comments were made comparing him to a current American Hollywood movie star:Tyrone Powers. But except for the hair, he couldn't see the resemblance. Both combed their thick black hair straight back without a part.

Manolo's hair was a secret source of pride; secret so he thought. His attention to good grooming and manners began and ended with his hair and he never could abide untidy hair in man or woman. It showed a lack of care. And woe to anyone who purposely messed with his hair!That individual would make that error only once.

In addition, he was trying his best to stay strong and pure; the "Ideal."

Committed to his Faith, he had been seriously considering the priesthood and it's celibacy demands. As the priests often reminded people:Any exercise in self control was as much about strength and dicipline as it was about The Church's moral expectations. In fact, it would be years before he engaged in any sexual activity. There were always cold showers and and other penitential endeavors to "quench any fire" . It wasn't long, however, before it became abundantly clear that celibacy was not for him. Life without women ?But he just adored them!

The months dragged as Paloma's health deteriorated. She seemed to be turning into a shadow lying on the bed. The family members attempted to stay calm and hopeful as they cared for her and Elena rarely left her bedside as she didn't want to lose any precious time with her dying daughter.

Fernando visited his daughter occasionally but his visits were short.

His anxiety, discomfort and pain were best shouldered away from the sickroom.

In the past, he had always managed to deny his painful emotions by finding some distraction and this situation was no different. He needed a distraction.

Three agonizing months went slowly by. One day, as Manolo neared his home, he heard his mother's cries. Rushing in, he found her at her usual post in his sister's bedroom.

"Manolo, quick, for the love of God...run...get the doctor!"

He shot out the door and ran the few miles to get Dr. Venancio. The doctor was home, thankfully. Grabbing his medical bag, he took off after the young man.

As Manolo rounded the corner to the Posada, he saw several women entering the house. Paloma's fiancee had been summoned as well and he knew then, that it was too late.

Entering the bedroom, his sister's body was already laid out on the floor for burial care to allow a proper burial position as rigor mortis set in. Friends and neighbors were doing their best to sooth his mother.

"But where is Papa?" he asked a neighbor.

"No one seems to know, Manolo," was the answer.

He decided to find his father." He's probably at the cafe." But when he got there, no one had seen his father that day. After checking all possible places, he returned home. An hour later, Fernando appeared. He didn't explain his whereabouts but went to console his wife.

Manolo could never forget the women's gossip the next day hoping it wasn't true but somehow knowing it was; Fernando had been 'distracted" by one of the servant girls.

"Do what you feel in your heart is right, for you will be criticized anyway...you'll be damned if you do and damned if you don't."

Eleanor Roosevelt

Chapter Fifteen

Completing his bacalaureate from the Institute, Manolo had some decisions to make. He had done very well in his studies and could now choose where he would go to complete his professional studies. Fortunate to have been taught by some dynamic professors who had recognised his interest and potential, his interest remained in history. He continued to devour books and it mattered little whether the subject was Spain's history, Ancient History or World History; he delighted in them all.

But there were some drawbacks to training as a history teacher. The Franco government had censured any and all material not officially approved by the government as well as the Roman Catholic Church. The resulting educational system was rife with ommissions and propaganda and anyone attempting any corrections was censured. Manolo began to realise he could not function under such conditions and began to search for another profession which would offer some autonomy and still challenge his intellect. He finally settled on the study of medicine.

"Well, if it's medicine, you must study at the University of Valencia. My family's close and can help you. Tio Ruben is doing well at his pharmacy and he can help with some of your bills...there is no other choice. We're just recovering from the war and don't have any money to support you anywhere else. So I'll call my brother tomorrow and let him know you'll be coming and you stay with him when you're not in classes." Fernando had decreed his son's future without delay or discussion.

"No, Papa. I'm not going to Valencia. I'm going to Madrid to study."

"Are you loco? We have no connections in Madrid, no family to help! In God's name, how will you live? No one has any money, don't you understand that?"

Beginning to feel irritated but strong and even more convinced of his decision, Manolo challenged his father." I realise that and I'm grateful for the offer, Papa, really I am but my mind is made up. I will go to University in Madrid and become a doctor."

"Bah! Cabezon...stubborn!"

Elena had wisely stayed out of the discussion. Out of respect for Fernando, she knew she would not openly challenge his authority yet her heart was with her son. She knew his ways and was not surprised at his decision. Certainly she preferred that he study in a place where family could easily support him; it would make her worry less. But she was proud of his drive and ambition and his need for independance as well as his courage to venture forward to follow his dreams.

"I'll save a little money and send it to him when I can. Fernando doesn't need to know."

Life as a student in Madrid had proved a lot tougher than Manolo had imagined. With little money and fewer prospects, he was completely on his own.

His small scholarship only paid for a tiny room in a small private boarding house and all other expenses had eaten up most of his meager savings. He managed to purchase a single meal coupon each day and chose dinner over other meals.

Sleeptime burned fewer calories and he could get through his day without a meal until the next evening.

Of course, wealthier people didn't go through this routine but pride and honor are often the first to suffer during deprivation. Circumstances aside, the young man made friends of all social stratas and found himself treated to a meal occasionally or a friendly beer after classes. Even so, hunger was a constant companion.

No money for books, he was at another distinct disadvantage. More time had to be spent in the Library reading and studying assignments but he rarely complained. After all, he had made his decision and by God, he would live with it and somehow succeed. The few pesetas that his mother sent him were helpful but weren't enough to buy even one textbook. He believed that one day, all his hard work and sacrifice would pay off and all this suffering would have been well worth it. He envisioned a life of reward with personal satisfaction in his profession and some financial rewards as well. He just needed to focus on his goal to become a medical doctor and keep his life simple. But sometimes Life has other plans.

Several months into his coursework, one of his fellow medical students, Casillas, approached him after classes had ended for the day. Manolo knew him slightly and found him friendly if a little too religious for his taste. It wasn't the first time Casillas had suggested Manolo join him for an evening but Manolo had been too busy but he couldn't find any excuse now and decided to join him as Casillas had suggested they go to an educational lecture.

"Hola! Manolo! I'll meet you at my residence at eight o'clock. It's on Calle Serano. I'll wait for you on the front steps."

"Your residence? Que?"

Smiling, Casillas nodded and walked back toward the medical school.

Evening came and true to his word, Casillas was waiting on the steps.

Joining him Manolo felt a bit uncomfortable as he was trying to imagine why the lecture was to be given at Casillas's residence. At that moment, a small grey haired woman opened the door and welcomed them in.

As the two entered the residence, Casillas led him into a large room with a lecturn and dozens of chair positioned as in a meeting. A large group of men, some from the University, were seated and listening to a formally dressed man deliver an address. Casillas motioned to Manolo to be seated and he began to listen. Virtues such as honor, faithfulness, truth, dicipline and devotion seemed to be the evening's topics as well as an emphasis on service to the Church.

Manolo didn't find the topics offensive in the least. But he did notice the lecturer referring to a book, ELCamino and several of the students seemed to have copies of the same book. Being at this lecture confirmed his idea of Casillas's religious bent but it was still an interesting talk. After an hour, the speaker; the man who seemed to be charge asked that anyone who had brought a guest to stand

and introduce him. Casillas didn't hesitate to present Manolo to the Director. After introductions, the Director approached the two.

"Senor Sanchez, your classmate Casillas here has been telling me some wonderful things about you...that you are a very serious man. You seem extremely well mannered, bright and like Casillas, committed to medicine. Am I correct in this?"

Embarrased with the attention, Manolo replied, " Si...Yes Senor. I am studying to be a doctor and hope to be a good one, God willing." He was at a sudden loss for words but remembered where he was, " All to serve God, of course."

"I'm glad to hear that. You see, not everyone feels that way. We are always on the lookout for sober, serious young men to join our little organization. It's a special holy order for God's work on earth. And when we find such individuals, those who are true believers in our Lord's work, we like to assist them anyway we can."

Now Manolo was really confused. What were they proposing he do? Join some kind of group?But all he wanted was to finish his studies!

"My son, Casillas will explain more at a later time. We want you to feel comfortable so take your time. Join us for our meetings a few times a week. And remember, it is only the best and most favored of God's people that are offered this chance."

Walking back to the University, Manolo began to question his friend. "Casillas, what the devil was that all about? What organization was he talking about ? Are you a member?"

"Manolo! Slow down! First things first. Just think about this evening. "Did you enjoy yourself?"

"Well, after a while, yes. I liked the dicipline and focus on education."

"OK, so listen, here's my stop. I'll see you sometimes in the next few days when we meet again and then we'll talk."

"All right. And thanks for an interesting evening. But, before I forget. You didn't answer me. I asked you if you were a member. What's it called?"

Smiling broadly, Casillas replied, " Yes I am a member and our group is called Opus Dei...the work of God."

As promised, Casillas met up with him at the University. He had a handful of documents all pertaining to the "special order" and encouraged him to read all of the material. He also invited Manolo to continue to attend the meetings with him and for several weeks, he did so. Casillas often reminded him that it was a great honor and privilidge to be a member as he would soon discover and he, Casillas, friend and sponsor would be happy to facillitate membership. He also reminded him that the order would take care of Manolo's rent, food and all other expenses. His worldly worries would cease so he could concentrate on his studies.

Sanchez was intrigued by Casillas's fervor. As he attended more meetings, he could see that the attendees were mostly University students of all diciplines as well as a few priests. The priests role seemed to be to direct the meetings and conversations and to answer any questions. Manolo liked the dicipline of the group and he certainly supported any good works but he became increasingly uneasy at it's emphasis on control and power. So many rules and regulations!

The strict behavior codes of intellectual rigor and allegience to the Church he could deal with. He had earlier toyed with the priesthood as a vocation and could envision himself as clergy except for one tiny issue:women. A life of celibacy?

Now that was the deal breaker! Now if he serve the order as a lay doctor, that he would consider. But when he discussed the idea with the directors of the Opus Dei, they all dismissed it out of hand. So why the increasing pressure to formally join the group? Why the hard sell? It was all getting a little creepy. Finally at one of his last meeings, he spoke to the priest in charge.

"Father, please try to understand. I really do appreciate that you find me so worthy. but the priesthood? It just isn't for me! Medicine is!"

"My son, we are not asking you to give up medicine...not at all! You continue your studies at University and we'll take care of the rest. Once you finish, we'll start your seminarian instruction."

"But I just want to be a regular doctor not a priest! Maybe a neurologist or psychiatrist so why isn't it possible for me to serve God as a physician?"

The priest seemed to losing all of his practiced calm demeanor. "Manolo, all of us feel that God is calling you to His priesthood. You are much too young to really know yourself. You need to trust us... God's messengers on earth. Think hard, my son, You could go far, very far indeed. Why, even as a professor at one of the universities! Think of the possibilities! They are endless and we will finance it all every step of the way! And think how proud your parents will be to have such a son!"

Momentarily silent, Manolo was thinking of the offer. Of course it would ease his life tremendously but he knew in his heart that it wasn't for him. But how to gently extricate himself from the group's control? Suddenly, it became very clear that it wasn't going to be easy. No, they had proved to be extremely tenacious group as he had experienced.

"Let me think about it, por favor...please."

Abruptly the priest turned away." I wouldn't challenge the will of God. No, that would be quite stupid, wouldn't you agree?" He wasn't smiling anymore.

The only way Manolo could lessen the pressure was to end any and all contact with the group's members. He remained cordial with Casillas as he didn't blame him for the mess. But in spite of all avoidance maneuvers, Opus Dei kept tabs on him. It seemed no matter where he was in the city, one of them was around. The situation was getting more than creepy, it was getting intolerable.

His classes were suffering, insomnia crept in and the psychological pressure had affected him so severely that he stopped attending some of his classes.

That helped alleviate some of the academic pressure but did nothing for his spiritual and emotional anguish. He had become a virtual prisoner in his room in an attempt to avoid any disturbing encounters with members of the group. Why couldn't they just leave him alone?

Casillas and another student could see that Manolo was suffering and approached him with a suggestion: Perhaps someone with higher authority could persuade the young medical student that God had called him to join Opus Dei? Would he consider meeting with someone, at least?

"Manolo, I know it's very difficult for you to accept that you really do have a higher vocation. You don't believe that now, I realise. But at least have the courtesy to meet with our founder and Spiritual Director. Father Josemaria Escriba is coming from Rome to Madrid next week. Will you let me see if I can set up a personal meeting with him?For your Soul's sake?"

Manolo found the request hard to refuse. After all, Casillas had remained friendly even though he had distanced himself from the friendship. Maybe he was missing something vital and a meeting with the Director would help put everything in perspective. Reluntantly he agreed.

Assuring Sanchez that he was making a wonderful decision, Casillas left to begin the process." I'll call on you when it's all arranged. You won't be sorry, Manolo!I promise!"

A few days later, an excited Casillas and another student called on Manolo.

"Unfortunately, Father Escriba is busy in Rome and cannot visit but we are blessed to have his deputy, Father Raimundo Panikkar. Father Panikkar is a true believer and believes we are the Militia Christi; the soldier of Christ. Like the first Christians! And you have a whole thirty minutes alone with him! We'll come by for you as we have the honor of escorting you. See you then!"

Watching the two students walk away, he noticed that they were grinning and shaking each others hands. It was almost as if they were congratulating themselves for some major accomplishment. How very odd!

The day quickly arrived when Manolo was scheduled for his audience with Father Panikkar. He remained anxious as he was escorted to the meeting and puzzled at his friends seeming euphoria." God, they're acting like I just won the lottery or something! I certainly don't feel so great!"

Manolo entered the large, dark room and gazed at the lone figure seated behind a desk. Obviously, this wasn't a casual interview. The man was short, slight of build and very dark. He did not smile at Sanchez as he motioned him to be seated. Panikkar seemed to take some time appraising the young medical student until he finally spoke. Beginning in a soft, slow voice, the interview began.

"So young man, I understand that you have been resistent to answering God's call ?"

"Well...it's not that, Father."

"Not that? What exactly would you call it, then? You have been hand picked by several men of God as someone who has been chosen. Do you understand that honor?Chosen to serve our Lord as one of Opus Dei...to do the Work of God!"

"But...but..."

"Well? Do you want to serve God?'

"Yes, Father, Of course."

"And don't you believe that the Lord's ordained sevants know better than you of how you should please the Lord?" Panikkar's voice began to rise.

"Yes, but..."

"It appears to me that your resistence is from some outside source then; something of the world and not your inner spirit. Lust? Ego?Perhaps something else? Fear the lord, my son. And listen well to His voice calling you."

The thirty minutes seemed to never end as Manolo was grilled and challenged by Father Panikkar. His stomach ached and head began to throb as the interrogation continued and his growing anxiety continued to mount.

Suddenly, the priest waved his hands and decreed, " That's enough!" Obviously the interview had ended. Panikkar seemed irritated as he frowned and Manolo lost little time as he made his way towards the exit.

"I've got to talk to someone before this drives me completely crazy! It's like they're trying to break me down.But who?" Manolo thought of a priest he had known in Albacete but who was now in Madrid, Father Garigos.

"Maybe he'll help steer me in the right direction."

He immediately called at the Rectory only to be told the the priest was at the church hearing confessions. Manolo decided to wait for as long as it took. He felt not only was his future at stake, but perhaps his very soul!An hour passed and Father Garigos emerged from the confessional.

"Manolo, what a pleasant surprise! What brings you to church?"

Anxious, Sanchez wasted no time as he explained his situation and the two spoke for over an hour." I can't function with all of this!My studies are practically nonexistent and I'm not eating or sleeping! I feel I'm going out of my mind!"

"Manolo, I'm glad you came to me. This is a dire situation indeed, and we both want you to make the right choices. I believe God doesn't want us to be miserable, so if you are willing, I will make arrangements for you to do a spiritual retreat at the Quatros Caminos. The convent is just outside of Madrid and in that place you may find the answers. And come see me afterwards, I may be able to assist you further."

Grateful for the assistance, he thanked the priest and made plans for his retreat. The spiritual retreat appeared simple and inane superficially, as days were spent attending meetings, community meals and contemplative walks.

At the close of the evening meal, everyone returned to their "cell" ; a small room simply furnished with a bed, chair, bureau and lamp. At this time one could pray, read or just meditate. The spiritual retreat lasted for three weeks.

A senior monk at the convent, Father Alonzo, made 'rounds" each evening making himself available to anyone who wanted some private talk and Manolo looked forward to his visits. He found the monk warm, engaging and easy to talk to. Alonzo had that rare, special gift:he actually listened.

"Manolo, you have your whole life ahead of you. Your heart has spoken to you and you have listened to it. In your heart, you know that the priesthood isn't for you so listen to your heart as that may be the voice of God!"

Feeling relieved and comfortable, Sanchez thanked the monk and he felt better than he had in months! During these few weeks, he had rid himself of insomnia, regained his appetite and lessened his anxiety. Most of all, he had learned to trust himself. He was now ready to reclaim his life. Packing his few belongings, he sought out the monk for a farewell.

"Father, I can't begin to thank you for all you've done. I'm ready to return to my studies and I'll follow your advice to keep away from the group. I'll cut all ties and ignore them. And I believe you when you say they'll eventually give up on me and leave me alone."

"One more thing, Manolo. Did you ever wonder about the others in your retreat group? Why they were here?"

"Well, yes...but I figured they all had other problems, none like mine."

The frowning monk looked directly at Sanchez."Without mentioning any names, over half of them were here for the same reason as you:the Opus Dei."

Back in Madrid, arrangements were made by Father Garigos to move Manolo into the Hispano-American Residence. There he would be less bothered by any unwanted intrusions. The other students in the Residence were a mixed group of students from Cuba, South and Central America as well as a few fellow Spaniards. He was amazed at how some of them were living as nothing was beyond their reach financially. But these students were from very wealthy families, unlike Manolo's. He had been extremely fortunate that Father Garigos was able to secure him a grant to cover room and board. In the new environment, Manolo thrived as he was able to borrow books from the National Library and from the other students.

Finally graduating from medical school, he had gained the title:Doctor of Medicine and Surgery. He fully realised that without Father Garigos's help, his life would have turned in another direction, and not the right one.

The next year was spent in mandatory military service as a "Second Lieutenant" and Military service completed, he returned to Madrid and secured a position at a private clinic as an emergency physician. His other duties included X-ray services and assisting in surgery and he would stay at this position for nearly three years.

Chapter Sixteen

Tired and sleep deprived, Manolo couldn't wait to return to his room for some much needed rest and quiet. He had been working forty eight hour shifts with twenty four hours off between now, for nearly three years but he had gotten used to the grueling and exhausing schedule. And all for room and board and six hundred pesetas a month; the equivalent of a mere fifteen dollars.

He had stayed at the Madrid clinic waiting for the owner and chief surgeon to make good on his promises but the promises of a raise and better working condidtions remained elusive. Each time he had approached the man to remind him of their agreement, he received the same response:manana...tomorrow.

Manolo was getting tired of the constant emergencies, X-rays and surgery. He knew he was good at the job, but his real interest lay in neurology and psychiatry. But in post Civil War Spain, he could not afford the thousands of pesetas required to complete the specialized training. At least this position paid him something during these hard times as other than his clinic income, he was penniless.

When not on duty and not sleeping, he spent his time at the National Library. If he wasn't devouring books by Sigmund Freud or Karen Horney, he was reading newspapers. The stories about America captured his attention as he read about the country's doctor shortage and his imagination took hold as he increasingly dared to dream; Maybe his future was in America!

Through his reading and conversations with his cousin Manolo Fernandez, he was well aware of the medical conditions in The States. The American goverment was advertising for and accepting foreign trained physicians to fill their post medical school Internships and

Residencies. The contracts were clear; one had to be a graduate of an approved medical school.

The applicant would then work and train in an American teaching hospital and in four years, return to his or her native country. If interested in US citizenship, one must leave the country for two year while the application was processed. If accepted, then one could return and stay. The final requirement was to have the ability to speak and understand the English language and that requirement was of the utmost importance, especially in medicine.

One of the three Manolos, Manolo Fernandez had secured a wonderful job at the Spanish Embassy in Washington DC. Married, he was happier in his secular life than he had ever imagine. Working as a Jesuit postulant years before in India had left him disappointed and worse; questioning his faith. But since leaving the order, he was surprised to find his faith returning. Not many knew, aside from a few people, of his amazing transition. Through family political connections and his fluency in the English language, he managed to land in the Spanish Embassy as a cultural Attache. His job primarily entailed arranging soirees and smoothing out any difficulties for visiting Spaniards. He loved his job and was happy to assist his doctor cousin to come train in America.

Aware that Sanchez had difficulty with the applications, he agreed to help with most of the paperwork leaving the doctor to attend to his travel plans and Sanchez was extremely grateful for his cousin's assistence.

Weekly letters kept the two in frequent contact until the week before Manolo's planned departure from Madrid. It was then that the conversation inevitably turned towards the Attache.

"But, last I heard, you were becoming a priest!"

"Ahh, Manolo. I'll tell you all about it when you arrive here. It's a bit complicated!"

"But what happened? And why are you being so mysterious?"

"Look. I'll fill you in when you come. Now stop! Let's get back to the important things:you coming! Everything in order?"

"Si...yes."

"Passport? Student visa?Plane ticket? Money?"

"Si...Si.. Si.. a little, poco."

"Don't worry about the money. Just have enough to get here and we'll figure out the rest later. Adios y Ve Con Dios!"

It didn't take long before Doctor's Hospital in Washington DC offered Sanchez a position an Intern in Medicine. The hospital's application committee had been impressed with his references and the enthusiasm displayed on the written essay explaining his reasons for continuing his education in The States. On paper, this young doctor was very impressive. The requisite formal interview had been disregarded considering the great distance and time constraints. So it wasn't until the day Manolo actually arrived at the hospital that everyone recognised a slight problem. He didn't speak or understand a word of English!

Getting everything in order for his trip to Anerica had been foremost on his mind. There was so much preparation! To further complicate matters, his longftime girlfriend had been pressuring him to" tie the knot" before he left for The States.

Maruha was a senior in nurses training at a hospital in Madrid and lived in the Sisters of Mercy convent attached to the hospital, From a respectable family, she was an attractive blonde and the two had dated one another, on and off, for a few years. Dating in 1950s Spain wasn't conducive to any form of real intimacy as cultural mores dictated prospective couples be under family supervision at all times; with few exceptions. An afternoon at the cinema, a meal or a coffee during the day were acceptable dates but that left little quiet, intimate time to emotionally explore one another's thoughts, dreams or expectations.

With almost constant supervision, it was nearly impossible to spend enough time to really get to know the other. The most one hoped for was a few stolen hugs and kisses, so matches were often made on superficial impressions, family recommendations or on pure impluse. Many couples found themselves legally bound to a spouse whom once they began married life together, didn't know or even like!

The only daughter of a police commissioner, Maruha and her father were avid supporters of the Franco regime. They considered themselves of a high social class and were often treated as such in their small city of Gandia. A bright woman, she carried herself with a patrician aire that masked inherent insecurity and barely hid her belief that by marrying Sanchez, she was lowering her social station while elevating his.

Of course, being a medical doctor certainly made him more acceptable and there was that little fact of his attractiveness. They had broken up a few times, always after he had the audacity to actually admit that, although he liked and admired her, he didn't really love her! Maruha would react with anger and tears but somehow, they eventually drifted back to one another. As she talked of marriage while Manolo listened, she initially agreed to his suggestion that they postpone marriage until he was settled in America, at which point he would send for her.

Maruha's mother watched as the engagement unfolded and gave a separate warning to each of them. She cautioned her daughter to marry before Manolo left as she was completely convinced that once there, he would change his mind.

"Maruha, Manolo has ambition and drive and once he gets to America, some girl will snap him up and that will be the last you'll hear from him. Are you sure marriage is wise? Are you sure you want to marry him? You marry him before he leaves."

"Oh Mama! Just stop interfering! We are engaged and he wouldn't break that if one hundred Hollywood starlets wanted him! He wouldn't jeopardize his honor so stay out of it."

To Manolo, she questioned," Are you sure about marriage now?I don't think you really know her, what she is like...I'd think more about this if I were you!"

Maruha's mother felt the match unsuitable based on both personalities.

"Manolo has too much passion and my Maruha has too little." Mother and daughter were embroiled in a highly conflictual relationship on even the best of days.

Maruha's mother wasn't the only one questioning the engagement. Elena had similiar doubts but for other reasons. She knew her son was a dreamer, full of imagination and passion. He should have a wife who shared some of those traits or at least understood and accepted them in him. Maruha seemed too formal, too concerned about her family's status and Elena wondered if she could fully support Manolo's dreams. In addition, and much more of a concern, she saw Maruha as too much like her own husband, Fernando, and that idea really saddened her.

Knowing her son's determination, she knew it was useless to attempt to change his mind with any pleading. But she did voice her concerns and make her feeling known. Manolo listen attentively and thanked her for her concern but he remained determined to go through with the marriage. Then he reminded her of an incident that had occurred several years earlier when he had been seriously considering the priesthood before choosing medicine.

Years earlier, Elena had made arragements with Manolo for a day visit in Madrid and as she had made all the arrangements, all Manolo had to do was to meet the train station. God willing, her plan would work and she sought some divine assistence by praying to the Catholic Virgin.

"Holy Mother, I ask for your intervention. I know you also had a Son who saddened you with His choices. But you loved Him so much that you could only watch as He suffered. Please let my son listen to me!" Three hours later, she was in Madrid.

"Mama! How wonderful to see you! Any problems with the trip?"

Kissing both cheeks, Elena held her son's face." My boy! No, No problema! But you are too thin! here, I brought you your favorite: a big tortiila and some fresh pan."

Grateful for the treats, he hugged his mother. No one made a tortilla as well as Elena Sanchez and he couldn't wait to eat it! But, first things first. Mama must be tired and would need something to eat and drink. He led her to a nearby cafe.

Finishing their lunch, Manolo asked her what she would like to do for the afternoon as they still had a few hours left before she needed to catch the train back to the family in Albacete.

"I want to see that show on the Grand Via. You must know which one, the one that everyone is talking about!"

"Mama! Surely you don't mean" The Follies" ?

"Yes! That's the one! That's where we'll go!"

"But Mama! You might be embarrassed by it! Hell, I'll be embarrassed by it! I've heard it's pretty racy."

"What! You think I haven't seen all that? And you! You're a medical student! Come on, let's go!"

Shaking his head in disbelief but knowing his mother's strong will, they went to the Theatre. It was just as he had been told and he was grateful that the dancers had kept their panties on, at least! He was acutely aware of his embarrassment at sitting in the Theatre watching half naked women; and with his mother! He couldn't wait for the show to end. It was the longest two hours he had ever spent.

"Well, that was educational! And didn't they dance beautifully? But I really didn't care for the comic. I didn't think he was very funny."

Suggesting they return to the cafe for some tapas before her train left, Manolo finally broached the subject. "Ok, Mama. What is this all about? And don't say "nothing." I know you too well!" His mother had something up her sleeve; an ulterior motive for taking him to the burlesque show.

"Manolo, I admit it. I wanted you to get an idea of what you'd be missing if you really did enter the priesthood. I also know you! You'll be miserable and very unhappy! You need to live life more! Have more experiences!"

His mother looked so forlorn as she spoke that he grabbed her in a huge hug and laughed, "Mama, I love you so much but you worry too much! I'm a man now and I have to choose my own path. Now go back home and stop worrying. I know what I'm doing and I know the priesthood isn't for me!"

Manolo watched as she boarded the train and until the train was well on it's way. Walking back to his room with his wonderful tortilla, he found himself laughing aloud, "I can't believe it! My own mother took me to my first "girlie show" !... my own mother!"

But the more Maruha thought about her mother's concerns, the more began to doubt her own plan. America was a very different culture and perhaps it was a better idea to marry before Manolo left. So a hasty marriage was arranged to take place at the chapel attached to the nurse's residence. The guests were few, just both family members and a few student friends of each. Manolo's marriage was not the most important issue for him as his attitude and subsequent behavior clearly showed.

He had left a crucial prerequisite for his nuptials until a few days before the planned ceremony. It had completely slipped his mind until his mother asked about it. He had not obtained a Certificate of Marriage from the Church. He needed to locate a priest to issue one, and quickly. But as he had not frequented any church in Madrid, he was not known to many. And as the Franco government had outlawed any civil unions, there was no way around it. Finally, he found a priest who could grant the Certificate.

"Senor Sanchez, since you are still a member of the diocese of Albacete, you must request a transfer to this Diocese of Madrid."

"OK. So how long will that take?"

"Well, we can start the process now and in several weeks, you should have it completed. And there is a fee."

"Several week! I'm getting married in a few days!" Manolo took a minute to think about the situation. Opening his wallet, he put it on the priest's desk.

"Here, take what you need to expedite it and just get it."

Nodding, the priest withdrew several hundred pesetas and did as he was asked. The Certificate was ready in two days.

The day of his wedding, he remembered another issue; he had forgotten to make his Confession. It was expected that a bride and groom make a formal confession to a priest and start their marriage fully contrite for past "sins" and once making an "Act of Contrition," be able to begin their married life absolved of any past trangressions. He found a priest to quickly hear his confesssion and hurried to the Chapel. But as he passed a men's clothing store, he realised he didn't have a tie.Dashing into the store, he purchased a tie, arriving at his wedding thirty minutes late. But at least he looked great! Why was getting married so complicated?

The honeymoon arrangements had been made without any of his input as Manolo just had too many things to do before he left for America. Maruha's family had booked the honeymoon destination. He didn't question the destination, although he did find it odd that they had chosen El Escorial. The ancient fortress was huge, cavernous and filled with Spain's deceased royalty. Not exactly the most romantic place to start a marriage!

A week was all the time allotted as each had to return to their respective responsibilities; Maruha to her nurse's training and Manolo to his travel plans. The week proved uneventful. There were no major coflicts but no bliss either. But he was embarrassed when the morning after their wedding night, the maid knocked on the door. She entered the room and quickly grabbed the bottom bed sheet as she engaged in a centuries old tradition of proudly displayed the virginal blood soiled sheet, making public the "purity" of the new bride.

"A hero is no braver than an ordinary man, but he is braver five minutes longer"

Ralph Waldo Emerson

Chapter Seventeen

Two weeks later he was on a plane bound for America. The first stop was New York City! His future plan seemed reasonable and he had no doubt it would easily unfold. Once his Internship started, giving him some time to get aclimated, he would then arrange a furnished apartment and finally send for his wife. Such a solid plan! What could possibly go wrong?

The plane landed at New York International on a bright, sunny morning and the exhausted but excited Sanchez de-planed full of high expectations. He gathered his two suitcases and then glancing at his ticket, proceeded to the Information Desk. He could make out some of the words as they were very similiar in Spanish. He needed to catch another plane; the one to Washington, that much he knew but from where? The size of the airport was completely overwhelming and at least ten times the size of Madrid's. It was just amazing!

Smiling, Sanchez approached the Information Desk. The lady seemed friendly enough so be began to ask for assistence.

"Buenas Dias, senorita. Por favor, podria usted decirma adonde consigno el avion a Washington DC?"

The woman looked up from her book and stared at him.

"I guess she didn't hear me, thought the doctor, Clearing his throat, he began again, " Buenas Dias, senorita...Por favor...Podria usted decirima adonde consigo el avion a Washington DC?"

The woman continued to stare for another minute and then, as if coming out of a trance, began to gesture and speak. She had recognised the Washington DC part, but nothing else. She guessed he may be speaking Spanish but she wasn't completely sure." Why do they keep sticking me over here in the International Terminal?I keep telling them that I only speak English!" So all she could do was to try to assist him.

"I'm sorry, sir, " she stumbled, " No understand-o Spanish. Please wait-o a moment while I get-to some help-o."

At this juncture, she pointed to a row of empty seats along a wall and motioned him to sit. Manolo understood that much but his anxiety began to rise when she picked up the microphone.

"This is the International Information Desk. We have a passenger who doesn't speak English and needs an interpreter. Please send someone immediately who speaks Spanish and can assist."

Fifteen excruciating minutes passed when a man wearing some kind of uniform with the words S-K-Y-C-A-P embroidered on his jacket and hat arrived at the Information Desk. The woman pointed to Manolo and the man approached.

"Buenas Dias, senor. How can I help you?"

He speaks Spanish!, Manolo smiled in relief. From his accent, he realised that the man was from Mexico but as his Spanish was very good so he showed the Skycap his ticket.

"Oh no, senor...You need to take the bus to LaGuardia, anotherairport and then get the plane to Washington." Manolo's anxiety returned. This "coming to America" was getting more complicated and he was feeling a little panicky at the idea of missing his plane.

He had very little money, just enough to pay for bus fare and a few meals and what if he got stuck here?He didn't know a soul and his only contact in the country was his cousin Manolo but he was in Washington!

Seeing the worried look on the foreigner, the Skycap announced, " Don't worry, I'll get you to the right place." And taking Manolo's bags, he added" Come on, we have plenty of time!"

As the two men walked away, the lady at the Information Desk added, "Welcomo to America, Cutipie!"

Once in Washington, Manolo quickly found his cousin waiting in the terminal and was more than a little relieved to finally see a familiar face. He didn't want to admit to anyone, least of all his cousin Fernandez, that his voyage had been so difficult. Bravado was second nature to any Castilian male.

"Manolo! You finally made it! How was the trip?" cried Fernandez in Spanish. They had not seen each other for a few years but they both felt that nothing had changed between them." He looks just the same, the lucky dog! And always so calm, so cool!" Even Fernandez had to admit that his cousin was a handsome man.

"Of course, I told you I would be here! The trip was long, that's all. Otherwise?No problema!"

"Well...together again! It's a pity the other Manolo couldn't be here as well. Then we'd be the three Manolos again! By the way, what's he up to these days?"

"Not much, unfortunately. He's still in exile in Mexico. You know how the political climate is."

"You're kidding! In exile? Hard to believe! But then, I always thought he'd end up in Russia writing long. boring philosophical books and waiting for the next People's Revolution!" Both men laughed.

"OK. Enough about him! Now you!What the hell happened to you? Were you defrocked or something?" Winking, Sanchez continued, " Or did you get caught carrying on with some nun?No one in the family could tell me anything!"

"That's because few people know. Defrocked?No, nothing so dramatic! I spent some years in India and found everything so disgusting! Not just the place, but the order as well. It really bothered me. Most of what I saw didn't make any sense! And you know? Most of the others felt as I did but insisted they needed to stick it out. They said they just didn't have the courage to leave."

"But I thought you were so religious! Everyone believed you would stay in the priesthood, even me! And you know how much I like the clergy."

"It wasn't an impulsive decision, Manolo. I just felt troubled all the time so I left. Call it a crisis of Faith, I don't know. But it got pretty ugly. Once I informed them that I wasn't going to take my final vows, they gave me a suit of clothes, a little money and then put me on a ship for Spain. They wanted very little to do with me after that and I became a persona non grata."

"Well, you seem to be doing well now! Here in America and with a pretty good job!. You know, I never told you but when I stayed with you that weekend in Alicante, you woke me up every night with your "devotions." I pretended I was asleep but I watched you as you knelt and whipped yourself. I thought you were a little religious fanatic but I did admire you for the dicipline. Me? I couldn't be celibate, that's just too much of a sacrifice." Fernandez laughed,

"As it turns out, it is for me too! Later, we'll all get together and you will meet my wife! Come on, let's grab a taxi to my apartment. You can stay with us until we find you a place. And I want to show you the capital of the free world! Fernandez was anxious to show off his knowledge of the "Capital City."

"Your wife? My goodness!"

As Sanchez had a few days before he needed to report to the hospital, he relished the idea of getting to know his new environment. He found, for the most part, the people were very open and friendly. Well mannered and extremely helpful, once someone realised the young doctor couldn't speak English, he or she would go out of the way to assist him. It didn't take long for him to gain the rudiments of the language but he was far from fluent. He would need much more preparation to function on his own.

The day finally came when he was to report to work. His cousin took the day off from the Embassy to accompany him just in case he needed a translater; a good move as it turned out. As he entered the hospital, his confidence grew.

Here were people from many nationalities and he could hear some Spanish! But having a family member close at hand to offer support bolstered his confidence.

OK, No problema. Time to meet the Internship Director and start my new life! he thought as he and Fernadez made their way to the office. They were warmly greeted by a pretty secretary who asked them to be seated.

"Which one of you gentlemen is Dr. Sanchez?"

At the mention of his name, Sanchez smiled broadly and offered his hand with a slight bow. "Encantado, senorita!"

A slight blush crept up her neck as she appraised this new Intern. She was barely aware that she was staring at him.

"And I am Manuel Fernandez, his cousin. I work at the Spanish Embassy and am here to assist my cousin as he doesn't speak much English."

This was a slight twisting of the truth!

"Can I offer you gentlemen some coffee?" The secretary had not taken her eyes off the doctor as she indulged her private thoughts." My God, he's adorable...a bit on the skinny side. But wait till the girls get a load of him!Reminds me of the movie star...what's his name?And no wedding ring! Very good, indeed!"

The two men thanked the secretary but declined her offer. Manolo was eager to start his Internship. He had often dreamed of this day, never really believing it would come to pass. And yet, here he stood, in America!

The inner door soon opened and out stepped the Director. A large man, he approached the two men and let his secretary make the introductions.

The pleasantries aside, the Director's attitude slowly changed from gregarious to somber as he began to realise his new Intern didn't speak English! How had that happen?His application didn't reflect that fact, but here he was. Now what?

"Well, at least his cousin can translate, " mused the Director.

"Please, Dr. Sanchez, Mr Fernandez. Come into my office so we can sort this all out."

Manolo's anxiety returned as his cousin explained the situation. It didn't look good. What if they decided to reject him? Send him back to Spain as a failure? End his dreams?These and other negative thoughts intruded upon and dampened his enthusiasm. "Well, there must be way to do this!"

The Director pulled no punches. He reviewed Sanchez's dossier and shook his head and his dismay and doubt were clear through Fernandez's translation.

"Dr. Sanchez. We are pleased that you have chosen Doctor's Hospital for your training. As you may be aware, we have a medical shortage here in The States and have encouraged good doctors from around the world to come and train to alleviate some of the need. In most cases, we have been very satisfied with our doctors and most have gone on for residencies in other American hospitals.

Now, your education is not in question and I can see that you're an affable young man. But, the language barrier is very serious. I want to be fair, so here is what I'm willing to do."

The Director continued to offer a plan to salvage Manolo's position. The conditions of the agreement would have to be acceptable to each party and if Manolo did not comply, he would forfeit his position and return to Spain. There were only two points. First: Manolo would work as an Intern but would be accompanied by a senior Resident physician as a supervisor and translator.

That way, he would continue his training without interruption and patient's safety would be ensured. Manolo readily agreed to the first condition. Second: but more challenging, he must learn, and quickly, a basic understanding and facility of the English language and enough to comprehend and communicate in a reasonable manner. Ok, he could do that!

"How long do I have to learn English?" asked Sanchez. Fernandez frowned as he told his cousin, "Three weeks."

"Three weeks? But how? And where?" After voicing his concerns, Manolo composed himself and informed the Director.

"Agreed! And thank you, sir. I want this position and I will succeed! Please tell me what I must do." Fernando looked incredulous.

"Man, are you loco?Learn English in three weeks?"

Manolo shot him a dark look so Fernandez stopped talking. The Director shook both men's hands and directed them out to his secretary.

"Miss Reed will make all the arrangements. You'll work mornings and each afternoon you will attent ESL, English as a Second Language classes. She'll enroll you this afternoon and you can start tomorrow morning, seven sharp! And Miss Reed will assist you with anything you may need."

"I certainly will." piped up the secretary, a little too enthusiastically.

The cousins left the office and lost in their own thoughts, neither spoke for a few minutes. Fernandez was not at all convinced that his cousin was up to this seemingly insurmountable task. Learn a new lanquage in just three weeks?

Impossible! But then, he didn't really know his cousin as well as he had thought, as he later discovered.

Watching the two men leave her office, a newly energized and grinning secretary returned to her desk." Oh yes, I certainly will give that Dr. Sanchez all the help he needs!"

The Director stuck his head out of his office once he heard the men leave.

Smirking, he addressed his secretary." Well, Miss Reed. looks like you have your work cut out for you! Now, please try to get Dr. Tyrone Powers signed up for ESL classes as soon as possibe. And try to stay a bit more professional, won't you?"

"Thats who he reminds me of! Tyrone Powers! What a dream-boat!"

"During the first period of a man's life, the greatest danger is not to take the risk."

Soren Kierkegaard

Chapter Eighteen

At five pm, Sanchez had just been relieved of his last forty eight hour shift.

He had been in Washington a little over two weeks and found himself tired at times, overwhelmed and more than a little bit lonely.

Letters from Maruha came regularly and he enjoyed them immensely but it didn't take the place of being with a live person. It was hard to express to anyone, his wife included, how difficult life had become. Learning English, the American medical system and the culture; it was all so very different! But as his challenges grew, so did his determination. He had spent every free moment learning English and in three weeks had become proficient enough to satisfy the Director's mandate. He was now convinced that nothing would get in the way of success. In addition, he really enjoyed being in this country; the freedom to do or say most anything without fear of reprisal, the abundance of food, the abundance of everything! Spain, was a different story. An embargo had been placed on Franco's Spain resulting in shortages of most necessities and hunger was common. The young intern began to seriously entertain the thought of staying in the US...and permanently.

He had not yet made any preparations for his wife's arrival but he convinced himself it was because he hadn't had any time. He rarely allowed himself to admit that he was ambivalent about her coming. Yes, they were married and he would support her and any children they might have but in his mind, she was unlike the women in Washington. These women were engaging, friendly and stimulated him as she had not. He tried to minimize and discount these unpleasant feelings but they continued to linger and his emotional conflict made him feel more and more uncomfortable.

"I married her and will do my best to provide her with what she needs. I'll be a good husband. Divorce is out of the question and against The Church and I will honor that. Besides, I bet once she comes here, it will be better. I'm probably just lonely."

He was gradually working more and more on his own and had made a few friends. Most of the hospital staff, from doctors and nurses to housekeeping seemed to like the Spanish intern, especially the women.

His European manners and foreign accent endeared him to the ladies.

Physically, it was difficult to identify him as any particular nationality as he was tall, a little on the thin side, with dark eyes and hair but his skin color was pale. He looked nothing like the doctors from South and Latin America and it wasn't until he started to speak, that his foreign origins became obvious. How many times had he heard the same exclamation, " But you don't look Spanish!" Obviously, these people didn't know that there were many varieties of skin and hair color in Spain. But most Americans did not make any distinction between the Latin countries and Spain and their very different cultures.

"Hey, Sanchez! I went to a party at your Embassy over the weekend! The food was great! Enchiladas, tacos, and tortillas. They were delicious!" One of the Residents, an American from Chicago, had approached him in the staff lounge.

Confused, he replied" Really? Enchiladas, tacos?What are they?" He remembered the wonderful tortillas his mother had made from potatoes and eggs but he had learned that here in The States they were known as omelets.

"Aw common Sanchez, you know what I'm talking about.Those rolled things filled with beans and hamburger!"

"Ahhh! Entiendo!Now I understand! You weren't in the Spanish Embassy, you were probably in the Mexican Embassy." And he proceeded to explain the food differences as the Resident's eyes started to glaze over.

He was just making conversation, he wasn't looking for a culinary lecture.Sanchez was always so damned serious! Hell, he didn't give a rat's ass about the differences...they all spoke Spanish, didn't they?

Changing the subject, the Resident reminded Sanchez that they were due on the wards in ten minutes. Every Intern was assigned a more senior doctor in training, a Resident Doctor, mostly for supervision and as a guide through the complex health care system. This particular Resident had been specifically chosen as he was bilingual. Washington has a substantial number of immigrants from Puerto Rico, Mexico and Cuba so his Spanish was a miasma of all of them.

As the two approached their patient's room, the Resident reviewed the case with Sanchez.

"Now, Miss Warren is one of our "regulars." She comes in every year fora "tune-up." She's extremely wealthy but a little on the neurotic side. Anyway, her family has donated millions to the hospital so we handle her with kid gloves. She's a looker, but at forty, a bit too long in the tooth for my taste. Here, look at her chart. All her labs are normal. We reviewed all her systems and found nothing. So now, you need to do a discharge interview and then write the discharge summary." He liked working with the Intern. Sanchez caught on quickly and could take alot of kidding." I'll be behind you in case you get into trouble."

Chart in hand, he quickly reviewed her admission. He couldn't find any presenting problem or diagnosis. "Are there alot of people like Miss Warren?"

"Well, you do realize Doctor's Hospital is private, don't you?"

Sanchez nodded in the affirmative, signally his comprehension.

"So, being private, we offer people a "million dollar work-up." Soup to nuts checkup at mucho dollars. Comprenda?Understand? They come in, stay a few days and we run all the tests. If we find something, we treat it. And if not, we give 'em a clean bill of health and send them on their way. They feel better, we get paid good money, and everybody goes home happy."

Manolo understood most of what he was being told, but what did soup and nuts have to do with anything? And kid gloves?. And what the Hell did the length of her teeth have to do with anything?Maybe some of those new American treatments he hadn't had time to read about ?

Confident that he had the vital information on this patient, Manolo entered the room, discreetly followed by the Resident. "Buenas...Good Morning, Miss Warren. How are you feeling today?"

Pointing to the Resident, she smiled, "Him, I know. Now, just who, pray tell, are you? My, my, my, handsome thing, aren't you?"

"I'm Dr. Sanchez, and I'll be taking care of your discharge. Any problems or questions before we start?"

"Go right ahead, doctor."

Grasping his stethoscope, he began the discharge physical. The woman seemed to be staring at him as he did the systems review but he continued using his best professional demeanor. He checked her vital signs, blood pressure, respirations and pulse and all were within normal limits. Next he checked her eyes. All results normal. Everything seemed to check out as normal.

"OK, Miss Warren, I'll write your discharge and you can leave anytime today. Will that suit you?"

"I've already contacted my chauffeur and he'll be here in a couple of hours to take me to the airport. Now, wouldn't you like to accompany me?"

"Que? Excuse me? What did you say?"

The woman motioned to the Resident. "Will you be a sweetie and explain to Dr. Gorgeous here what I'm offering him?"

Stepping forward, the Resident could no longer contain his amusement.

Turning to Sanchez, "You don't have a clue, do you?"

"Por favor, please. Explain what she asked and why is it funny?" Manolo knew that the woman had been flirtateous throughout the physical exam but he had just taken that in stride. It meant nothing and he hadn't responded.

"Dr. Sanchez, Miss Warren has invited you to accompany her on her trip. She says that she could use a "doctor." The resident burst out laughing.

Still confused, Sanchez replied, "But where? Where does she need a doctor?"

"Miami!" Do you get it now?" What was with this guy, all these dames falling all over him?

Blushing, Manolo did. Surely she was joking. " Senora, I thank you for your kind offer, but I must decline."

"Your loss, sweetie."

Following the still laughing Resident out of the room, he mumbled to himself,"I guess I still have alot to learn from these American women! What next?"

The Intern smiled to himself as he thought about all the attractive women that worked at the hospital. It didn't help that they were so friendly and engaging.

He made mental comparisons with the women in Spain. Attractive, some, but social mores dictated the males were to pursue and the females to allow the pursuit. Compared to ladies in Spain, the American women would be considered "loose" or agressive. The cultural reality was that Washington was a mecca for thousands of young women who had come to work for the many politicians and offices in the Federal government. They, too had come to make their own fortunes. With so many pretty women in the city, it was very easy for any young man to attract attention, wanted or not. And these women were more open with their wants and needs, making things much easier for the men. Although he found this attitude refreshing he was still a little uncomfortable with this different cultural attitude and a little bit frightened.

All of these thoughts and feelings were rolling around in his mind as he walked the several blocks to his room. Suddenly, he heard a woman's voice.

He was momentarily a little confused as he shook himself out of his daydreams.

"Doctor! Doctor Sanchez, Up here!"

Manolo looked up to a second floor balcony and saw a young woman wrapped in a large blanket. He vaguely recognized her from somewhere, from the hospital most likely, but in his fatigue, couldn't quite place her.

"Doctor, please, I need you.Please come!"

Too tired to fully comprehend the situation but recognizing a plea for help, he nodded and wearily climbed to the second floor. By now, expecting an emergency, his adrenalin was pumping and he was energized. As he reached the apartment, he noticed the door had been partly closed and the woman had stepped back behind it.

"Hello ?Miss? What's the problem?" he asked as he walked in and closed the door behind him. No one seemed to be there!

"Miss? I said," Do you need a doctor?"

At that moment, the woman appeared from the other room except this time, she wasn't wrapped in the blanket. She was stark naked!

Manolo was shocked at the sight of the young woman. This was certainly not what he expected to find when he was climbing the stairway. Recognition began to filter into his mind as he thought,

"Oh, she's the attractive girl who works in the hospital cafeteria! My God, she's gorgeous!"

"But I DO.I DO need a doctor. And badly!"

The lovely lady sauntered over to Sanchez and put her arms around him.

"So badly...."

Manolo smiled," Well, I guess this is an emergency!

"I can resist anything but Temptation."
Oscar Wilde

Chapter Nineteen

After a few months, the doctor had begun to settle into a routine. He was still living in a small room near the hospital and spending his free time immersed in the study of English. Once in awhile, he explored the city and he remained excited about this new country; he could hardly wait to see more of it.

Securing an apartment for Maruha remained elusive. He fully intended to get it :manana. There was just too much to do, more interesting things that kept catching his interest. And the nurses! Why some were just so kind and helpful and very attractive. Like Miss Fletcher, for instance.

Nan Fletcher had been working at Doctor's Hospital for the better part of five years. Few people would have said she looked her thirty five years and most of the hospital staff believed her to be in her late twenties. Blonde and buxom, she attracted a lot of attention from men.

The doctors at the hospital were no exception. Everyone at the hospital was aware that she had accepted a marriage offer from a wealthy oil tycoon whom she had met at a party while her fiancee was in Washington on business and had returned to his home in Texas. The mutually agreed plan was for her to join him in a few months. That was the agreement. A divorcee, she had decided that until her marriage, how and with whom she spent her time was her own affair.

"Congratulations, Sanchez!" The Chief Resident approached him in the cafeteria. He had arrived from Colombia a few years earlier and was comfortable with both English and Spanish.

"Que, what? Congratulations?Porque? Why?" Manolo was truly confused. What in Hell did I miss now? He was aware that his lack of language skills and ignorance of much of American culture often got him into "questionable situations" but his lack of guile and his likability excused many sins. He wracked his brain trying to remember what the Chief was referring to.

Although known for his good medical skills, the Chief was mostly admired for escorting and dating Miss Fletcher.

"Oh, come on! Don't play innocent! I don't know how you did it but Miss Fletcher won't give me the time of day."

"What in the world does that have to with me? I have nothing to do with that." Manolo was getting a little perturbed.

"Oh? Maybe not now, but I give you a couple of days." And with that prediction the Chief slapped him on the back and strode off.

"What the hell?" Now he was really confused. Miss Fletcher had been very helpful with learning the EKG machine. She did spend extra time with him and he marveled at her patience. She was certainly a beauty but she was never openly flirtatious... or was she? The more he tried to make some sense of the situation, the more miserable he felt. " I'm just going to pretend that the Chief didn't say anything."

A few days went by and as predicted, Miss Fletcher approached the Intern. "Dr. Sanchez, can I buy you a coffee?" Surprised but honored with her forward request, the Intern blushed.

"Pero...but...Miss Fletcher.... I should ask you...the lady" He was making great strides in conversing in English but continued to struggle, and it was too easy to fall back to familiar European customs.

Laughing, Miss Fletcher smiled. "Doctor, here we aren't so formal. It's not unusual for a woman to initiate something, especially when they find the man interesting and attractive."

"Gracias...thank you, Miss Fletcher. Coffee would be great." It didn't take long before Manolo was comfortable with the nurse. She helped him familiarize himself with the culture's norms and expectations. Spending most of their free time together assuaged much of Manolo's loneliness and he found her company enjoyable and relaxing. He was very open and forthcoming about his marital status and made it clear that his wife would be joining him in a few months.

Nonplussed, Miss Fletcher continued to assist him in furnishing Maruha's new home.

"Look. We both are "taken" as such, you with your wife, me with my fiancee but that doesn't mean we can't make the most of our time together!I really like you, Manolo and I think you like me as well. So relax!"

"I do like you! You've been so very kind and helpful And I can't begin to tell you how wonderful you've been."

"You know what I think?I think we have both been working too hard. I need a break and so do you. Have you been to up Baltimore yet ?"

"Not yet, I want to visit that city. I hear lots of good things about it; the waterfront.... the seafood..."

"Ok, then! I'll pick you up on Saturday morning. Say nine am ?And I'll show you Baltimore! We can have lunch, do a little shopping for your apartment and have dinner at the Waterfront Cafe and then come back. Sound like a good day?"

"I'd like that! Yes, I really appreciate your friendship."

"And you can stop calling me "Miss Fletcher, " My name is Nan."

"OK, Miss Flet...... I mean, Nan."

As she walked out of the cafeteria and back to her office, she was smiling broadly and thought, " I think, Dr. Manolo, come Saturday you'll see just how "helpful" I can be!"

Saturday morning finally arrived and Sanchez was surprised at his growing anticipation. Looking forward to discovering a new city was just a small part of his excitement. He was looking forward to spending the whole day with a lovely lady. She had become a valuable friend to him and he was enormously grateful for her attentions. And thanks to Miss Fletcher, his conversational skills had improved as had his comfort level. She had found a way to make him laugh at his many language errors and seemed to really enjoy his company.

Recognizing his growing attraction to her, he nevertheless insisted on treating her as a lady and refused to behave otherwise. He would not risk her good feelings by acting like an affection starved idiot.

He heard her drive up and honk and was down the stairs in a flash. She looked smashing behind the wheel! Her blonde hair peeking out from beneath a white sunhat and dressed in a haltertop blue dress. He had never seen her other than in her nurse's uniforms and the contrast took his breath away. The dress emphasized her stunning body.

Getting into the passenger seat, Manolo's appreciation was obvious. He tried to appear nonchalant but he had trouble taking his eyes off her. To distract himself, he looked into the back seat.

Noticing a large blanket crammed next to some bags, he inquired, " Do you always carry a blanket in your car?"

"Oh, you never know when it will come in handy!"

A blanket? In August? It's so damn hot now! Why would we need a blanket? Maybe it's just one of those American quirks, he thought.

As they drove into Baltimore, Miss Fletcher suggested they check out a building. There was something there she was sure he would like. Parking the car, she instructed him to grab the blanket. Manolo did as requested and followed her into the building. It looked completely empty and abandoned. How odd!

"This will do!" Taking the blanket from him, she spread it on the floor.

Not sure of himself, Manolo just stood as she removed her hat and then her dress. Walking up to him, she put her arms around him and gave him a long, sensuous kiss. There was no queston now, what the blanket was for and he started to laugh." Well, Doctor, are you just going to stand there laughing or shall we see just how nice our time here can be?"

They returned to Washington late that evening, exhausted but happy. It had proved to be an extremely interesting day. As she dropped him at his apartment, she playfully kissed him." So, how did you like Baltimore?"

"I...I don't know what to say! It certainly is an exciting city.Just full of surprises! Wonderful surprises, but I'm exhausted! I don't think I have the stamina to see anymore of it." They both laughed at the joke.

"I figure we christened that blanket at least five times, wouldn't you agree? And I must say, I had a wonderful time. Let's do it again!"

"I can't "moaned the doctor," You'll kill me!" He really was tired and sore. That much" activity" after awhile, would exhaust even the strongest libido!

"Poor boy! Not now, silly! You wore me out too! Get some rest and I'll see you at work tomorrow! And you should really call me Nan. Miss Fletcher is far too formal now that we know each other so much better."

Slowly walking up the apartment steps, he burst out laughing. Yes, he had been to Baltimore for the day. It was a pity he had only seen several abandoned buildings. My God, these American women were something!

While at the hospital, the two kept their relationship strictly professional.

Off duty, she continued to help him with the language and the preparations for Maruha and neither held any illusion that once his wife came, the relationship, would radically change.

Nan Fletcher's upcoming marriage was only a few months away as well. She planned to fly to Houston, get married, then return to Washington to finish packing for her final move to Texas. The weeks seemed to fly by as their time together was rapidly drawing to a close..

"Well, my dear Manolo, I must leave for Texas in a few days. I'll certainly miss you and our "adventures" ! But I'll be back in a few weeks to finalize my move. I might see you then."

"Funny, I just got a letter from my wife. She comes next week!"

"Such good timing, Manolo!Your apartment is all set. You've settled in at the hospital and made some good friends. You'll be fine!"

"Si...yes, thanks to you! I don't know how I would have managed without you, honestly!"

"Hey, we had some great times!You're a wonderful guy and I hope your wife appreciates that. We both need to get on with our lives and like I said, I know you'll be fine!"

As they hugged and kissed for the last time, Manolo couldn't help thinking, "She's right. And I wish her the best with her life. I am doing well, thanks mostly to her. But now, how well will I do with Maruha?"

"If you tell the truth, you don't have to remember anything."

Mark Twain

Chapter Twenty

Continuing to work at Doctor's Hospital and remaining focused on improving his English, Manolo spent any free time exploring life in Washington.

One day, while waiting for a bus he noticed another young man standing nearby. He glanced at his well tailored suit and beautiful shoes." Must be some top official, " he surmized. The man slowly approached.

"Buenas Dias, senor." Recognizing a regional Spanish accent, Manolo was taken aback; other than at the Embassy, there weren't too many people from Spain in Washington.

"Buenas Dias, Senor, " smiled Manolo.

"Have you been in Washington long?"

The two men began a conversation as the man began to ask many questions of Manolo. What brought him to Washington? What, if any plans had he after his Internship? And his future?So many questions!

Watching the bus approach, the man graciously handed Manolo his business card.

"Take this, my friend. You never know when you may need it."

Manolo accepted the card and placed it in his breast pocket. He would look at it later. The bus stopped and Manolo prepared to board. Turning slightly, he wanted to ask the man another question. But the man was walking away from the bus stop and at a rapid pace. During the short encounter, Sanchez had introduced himself but strangely, the man did not do likewise. It was almost as if the man had already known his name!Curious.What a bizarre coincidence!

And how strange that he didn't board the bus. It was almost as if he had been waiting for someone.

Seated and readying himself for the twenty minute ride, he reached into his pocket and retrieved the business card. Shock and anxiety gripped him as he read the gold lettering :Office of The Opus Dei.

Maruha Sanchez had better luck with her arrival than had her husband. Aware of Manolo's initial trouble, she would not be so foolish or shortsighted.

"I swear, he just doesn't plan anything!" She had arranged for an interpreter as soon as she landed in New York. Manolo met her in the Washington Airport.

Sanchez was surprised at his pleasure at seeing her. Again, he was reminded of her attractiveness and had made the decision to be a faithful, good husband to Maruha and leave Nan Fletcher in the past, especially emotionally. Time to start anew. Besides, Maruha couldn't possibly find out about his indiscretion, Miss Fletcher was in Texas by now. He did miss her terribly but that was the price he must to pay. His marriage awaited him and must come first.

Mixed feelings plagued Maruha as she settled into her new apartment. She much preferred the familiar surroundings of Madrid but knowing they would return in a few years after her husband's training kept her spirits up. Her only socialization revolved around Manolo's cousin and wife.

A month went by and Manolo returned home weary from his shift. Since Miss Fletcher's departure, he had thrown himself further into his hospital duties, leaving little time for Maruha. She quickly realized, talking with the other wives, that an Intern's wife was a very lonely one. Socializing, other than getting together at each others places for a meal was extremely rare, so when Manolo announced that they had been invited to an evening soiree at the Hispanic - American Center her reaction was sheer delight.

At last a chance to get dressed up, meet some "proper" people and communicate in her native language. She would get to talk about herself and esteemed family in Spain. Why in Spain, they all knew who she was! She wasn't just anybody. She was the daughter of Gandia's chief of police!

Evenings at the Center were an opportunity to honor the national celebrations of the Hispanic-American countries and a time for guests from other countries to learn something new about each country.

The Sanchezs were seated in the auditorium waiting for the program to begin. Next to them were two empty seats and as Manolo looked up, he saw two familiar faces; a man from the Spanish Embassy and he was escorting Miss Fletcher!

Introductions were at hand. Comfortable in social situations, the Attachee began as he glanced at Miss Fletcher, "May I introduce Dr. and his wife, Senora Sanchez?"

"Oh, I know Dr. Sanchez from the hospital." replied Miss Fletcher, "But I have not had the pleasure of meeting Mrs. Sanchez. How do you do! Welcome!"

Manolo dared not look directly at Miss Fletcher, for fear that his feelings might surface in full mode. But what what she doing here?He was completely flummoxed and speechless.

Seeing her husband momentarily uneasy, Maruha nudged her husband "Manolo..."

"Ahhhh...Miss Fletcher and I used to work together at the hospital, Maruha. She was a great teacher, of many things." For the first time, he looked directly at the nurse." I heard you got married. Congratulations."

"Yes, thank you! We cut our honeymoon short as I have so much packing left here in the city that we both thought it would be wiser for me to spend this week organizing my move to Houston."

"So your husband is still in Texas?"

"Of course! I need to tie up some loose ends here and then I'll be joining him...permanently." No one said a word. Interjecting the "pregnant pause," the Attache broke the uncomfortable silence.

Everyone shook hands and sat and the conversation soon became lively as the Attachee, Maruha and Miss Fletcher exchanged tales of travel difficulties and opinions on life in America. On the surface, the party of four appeared cordial and comfortable, however, feelings of anxiety were building in all but the Attachee. He was blissfully ignorant of his companions' complex and interwovan relationships.

Miss Fletcher seemed relaxed and at ease, displaying no obvious signs of having anything other than a casual professional relationship with the Intern. She treated her date in the same manner; cordial, friendly but with no indication of any prior intimacy. Her frequent smiles directed at Manolo, and his directed to her were not noticed by anyone in the group with one exception: Maruha.

Maruha became unusually quiet. She was not known as a retiring personality and was used to talking incessantly to anyone who would listen. Inevitably, no matter the subject matter, she would turn the conversation back to herself, her personal accomplishments and her esteemed Spanish geneology.

Most aquaintences would listen politely at first but soon, growing tired of the self involved, repetitive conversation and found themselves drifting away toward some peace and quiet. Eventually, with her husband's help, she recognised her maladaptive behavior but as all therapists know, insight is just half the battle. Behavior change is the other. And Maruha's behavior did not change.

Often, this attitude struck aquaintances as haughty, bordering on arrogant but few understood that it served to mask an underlying anxiety and low self esteem. Convinced of her own superiority, she would not allow herself to be upstaged by her doctor husband. In her estimation, she had married below her station and he should be grateful that she lowered herself to marry him in the first place. For that, he should be very grateful. She reminded him of that "fact" and often.

"Is anything wrong?"

"No, Manolo. But I was going to ask you the same thing. You changed when that woman and her date sat down. You looked like you had seen a ghost."

"It's nothing, I was just surprised to see them, that's all."

"Hmmmnn...If I didn't know any better, I would say that you were jealous."

"Preposterous!" Manolo recovered quickly. He realized his reaction was more intense than intended. He would put an end to this conversation, and now.

It was the safest position to take. He knew that Maruha was capable of embarrassing public outbursts and he had seen his share in Madrid. He wasn't going to risk that. Not here, certainly.

Perhaps she was just testing him, trying to get a reaction from him. He wouldn't put it past her. Initially he had placidly accepted her histrionics. In actuality she had been his first real girlfriend and other than the his female relatives, he was woefully ignorant of normal female cognitions and behaviors.

Over the past several months, he gained much exposure to the" fairer sex "and in many different roles. He came to a startling realization: Maruha's behavior was not usual, not in the least.

Deciding he would take the bull by the horns, he informed her that he would no longer accept or tolerate any of her hysterical maniplulations. His expectations were clear:She was to behave properly and reasonably, especially as a doctor's wife.

"Maruha, we'll discuss this when we get home, now please, just drop it" Sanchez found his embarrassment mounting.

His wife wisely decided to hold onto her suspicions and wait until they returned home to get to the truth.

Both were silent as the cab drove through the night. As their apartment was just several blocks from The Center, the quiet was short lived. Fuming, Maruha exploded once inside the door." Just who is that woman?"

"What woman? You met several tonight..."

"Don't play stupid.I know you're not, and I certainly am not! That nurse, Miss Fletcher. I watched you and her and don't insult my intelligence by denying that she's nothing more than a "friend". I'm not blind! I knew it. Damnit. I knew I couldn't trust you!"

Her rapid fire accusations were matched in volume and pitch. Her face had turned such a deep purple, that all Manolo could think about was an impending stroke or heart attack.

"Please, calma...calm down! Deep breaths...You'll have a stroke!"

"And it would be all your fault, too!" But, in spite of her highly charged emotional state, she complied and took some deep breaths.

Seeing her settling, he made a decision. He would be completely honest with her. Now that she was here and Miss Fletcher was gone out of his life, he vowed to make a new beginning with Maruha. It would be hard, but honesty really was the best policy.

"OK. Now, let's discuss this as two rational adults. I will answer your questions as honestly as I can. Then can we get on with our marriage. Agreed?"

"Agreed...." She was calmer, but only slightly." That woman is more than a "friend," isn't she?" Maruha was eyeing him closely, waiting for any telltale body language that would betray her husband.

"Was. and listen to me..... Was. She is married now and on her way to Texas. You are here and we need to start fresh."

"Was? Was???" Manolo could hardly hear the words for all her screeching." You slept with her, didn't you, you Bastard!"

"Maruha, it was nothing! I was lonely. She was lonely...it just happened. And it's over! I'm sorry if you're hurt but I wanted to be honest with you...you asked! I said...it meant nothing!"

The Intern hoped his confession sounded sincere. He was truly sorry for causing his wife such distress, he really was, but he couldn't bring himself to disparage Miss Fletcher. He had only fond memories of her and wished her well in her new life. At least he knew enough to keep those feelings to himself.

"Nothing? You make love to a woman and it means NOTHING!!! You Bastard. I suppose I mean nothing either?" she screamed.

"Maruha, Maruha...you're my wife, I married you. Can't you forgive me so we can start over?" He continued petitioning her. He could see that she was still enraged, but her agitation seemed to be lessening.

"I can't believe you would do this...and to ME! I never should have married someone beneath me. Your lower class morals are obvious now. I'll never forgive you! You dared do this to me!" At that last invective, she stomped into the bedroom." And don't you dare come near me, you...you..".

Sitting in the livingroom, Manolo had few options. Of course he wouldn't bother her. That wouldn't be the behavior of a gentleman. He decided to bunk on the sofa for the night. Tomorrow would bring another battle, of that he was positive." Thank God I have a day off from the hospital. I don't think I could deal with that drama as well as Maruha's" and closing his eyes, he fell into a dreamless sleep.

Morning came, along with Maruha's silence. Her husband realized the best course of action was to pretend nothing had happened. He was confident that once the dust settled from last night's confrontation, they would continue on the chosen path.

"Buenas Dias, Maruha.... I made some coffee. Would you like a cup?" He tried to smile and act as if nothing was wrong as he offered a cup of the brew.

Lighting her first morning cigarette, she warily looked at him.

"Si.. Yes,... gracias" Manolo joined her in a smoke. "What would you like to do today? I can show you the White House or we could so some shopping. What do you say?"

He really did long to show her around her new home. He wanted her to become as familiar and comfortable with the city as he had become. Actually, he was more than proud, he was beginning to enjoy his surroundings. "Such a prosperous and exciting place. And we can think and believe anything we choose and no one, no one can take that from us! Such freedom!"

Still smarting from last night's confession, Maruha didn't care what the hell they did and angrily told him so. She felt trapped and confused. Her honor had been tested. He had broken his marriage vows, and so soon! She was still livid and stunned that he had the very nerve to do this to her.

On the other hand she was no idiot. Not possessing means or language, she was utterly dependent on her husband. In America for a single week and already she hated it. She could not bring herself to admit, certainly not to Manolo, that she had few real options. The reality was that returning to Spain offered more risks, as she would be judged a failure.

Divorce was not an option; her religion had closed off that choice. She would be a woman in Limbo. No other marriage offers would be forthcoming and a woman in that position would live out her life as the burdensome maiden Tia, Aunt. Worse, she would always be dependent, financially and otherwise, on the generosity of her family. Such humiliation.

"You choose, Manolo, I don't feel like making any decisions. After last night, I'm just too tired... obviously."

"OK, let me show you the Capitol and the White House. Believe it or not, they'll show us around. We can walk right in! Everything is so open and free!"

Manolo mistook her somber mood for forgiveness and maybe even acceptance of his indiscretion. Thinking the crisis was over, if not forgotten, he continued in the conversation.

Bur Manolo watched as his wife's face changed color, from pink to red to a light purple. Like an active volcano, Mt. Maruha erupted, her voice rising higher and higher, "Bastard".

"I think I'll just go get a paper." Shaking his head as he escaped from his wife's wrath, he mumbled to himself,"When will I learn to keep my mouth shut and just quit while I'm ahead ? Perhaps complete honesty in a marriage wasn't such a good idea, after all... And funny, I never did call her Nan."

Years Later..........

Manolo and Maruha eventually agreed to a truce and continued on wth their lives. After completing his residency, Manolo took advanced training in Psychiatry and the family moved to Kentucky. Blessed with two healthy boys, the couple finally settled into a routine and did their best to raise a family.

Manolo was eventually offered a lucrative position at Southern State Hospital where he soon became Chief of Staff. Marriage aside, both parents doted on the boys and were pleased that both had become successful professionals, enjoyed happy marriages and had presented them with four healthy grandchildren.

Inspite of continued marital discord and both parties disatisfaction, the marriage continued to bump along for almost thirty years. Finally, however, Manolo and Maruha called it quits, separated and divorced in 1991. Maruha quietly withdrew from her active social life and Manolo continued his medical practice at Southern State Hospital until he retired: once...then twice...Neither remarried.

"I don't believe in accidents. There are only encounters in history. There are no accidents."

Pablo Picasso

CHAPER TWENTY ONE

For the first time in his life, Manuel was at a loss as to his future. Through out his last retirement, any plans he made somehow fell together without much forethought. His life had certainly been "challenging," to use the modern jargon, but problems and difficulties did not lessen just because one renamed them. The psychiatrist quietly laughed to himself.

"Well, it's not like this is a new idea; I've retired twice before!" Sanchez had "traditionally" retired two years earlier after nearly thirty years of service to one of the country's oldest clinical mental facilities; Southern State Hospital. After a year of part time clinic work, he felt restless, bored and probably a little depressed. It was quite by accident that while he was at the local bank, he ran into SSH's superintendent:Joe Foster.

"Big Joe" Foster was a giant of a man and at six feet, six inches, his large frame filled any doorway. His aids joked that he looked like a smaller version of a certain Italian tenor but couldn't carry a tune in a bucket. At the age of forty five, he had managed to work his way up the professional ladder from social worker to superintendent of the hospital and his mastery of politics was legendary as well as formidable.

Only a few close friends were aware that Big Joe carried a copy of Machiavelli's The Prince in his briefcase. He had studied it well and often referred to it as his "Bible." Although possessed of a keen intelligience, Foster's meteoric rise to power was aided all the way by a certain savvy and nurturing his political associations had become his forte.

"Dr. Sanchez! How's retirement?"

"Oh, it's all right. Can't complain."

"Well, have I got a deal for you! Would you be interested in coming back, say half time! Maybe mornings?No on call, of course, straight Monday through Friday. What do you say? We really do need you. These new docs are a tad unreliable; always wanting more time off and then when they work for a few years and then leave and go off to start a practice. But you. Why you're "old guard!"

Dr. Sanchez was taken by surprise but readily agreed. He really did miss the patients and the bustle of the Admissions Unit and by working just mornings, he could still have time and energy for his other interests.

"Mr. Foster, you have yourself a deal. When do you need me?"

"Yesterday!" laughed the superintendent, " But I'll tell Human Resources to give you a call later today so you can come in and start early next week. That OK with you?"

"Sounds fine. So I'll see you next week! And thank you."

"Oh Hell no, thank you, Dr. Sanchez!"

Although the hospital managed to lure a few more foreign trained medical doctors for staffing, Sanchez's experience and historical perspective proved invaluable to the less tested psychiatrists. Besides, since he wasn't really ready to accept a permanent retirement, the contract suited him just fine.

Socially, since his divorce years earlier, he maintained a good relationship with his two sons; his ex-wife was another issue. He would have preferred to keep a cordial relationship with her as well. He didn't hold any hard feelings towards her or her initiation of the divorce as he had not exactly behaved in an exemplary fashion during the marriage, but he had truly not meant to hurt anyone.

It had been obvious that they had been badly mismatched; ill suited as a couple and to that, even Maruha had to eventually agree. In the spirit of fair play, Manolo had been generous and consistent with alimony payments. In spite of his encouragement, especially after their sons were grown, she never utilized her training and refused to work outside of the home. Consequently, she had few financial resources and all in all, he didn't want to see her in lanquishing in poverty.

Other than his enjoyable but infrequent visits from his sons, daughters-in -law and grandchildren, Manolo had a sort of "lady friend." A retired nurse, her main interest was exotic travel; an interest he did not share. He enjoyed her company but she didn't sustain any real excitement or passion and after a few hours, he grew tired of her company. She had continued to suggest that they "cement" the relationship and he move in with her. His standard answer was "we'll see." He would like to continue the relationship but he had no intention of actually living with the woman or anyone for that matter. He believed himself to be too old for that sort of foolishment.

"Insanity...a perfectly rational adjustment to an insane world."

R. D. Laing

Chapter Twenty Two

The blow to his face seemed to come from nowhere adding to the stress of the assault. Dr. Sanchez stood paralyzed as the young patient, Dwayne, fled to a corner of the Day Room and lay in a crouched, defensive position.

The ward staff hurried Sanchez out to the staff station, pushing the alarm button as they went. The large red buttons were strategically placed throughout the facility as a safety precaution and the boxes were all computerized to light up a particular area. Anytime one was pushed, designated staff, usually male psychiatric aides, ran to the site. The rapid response was slowed only by the series of locked doors. Every single door, exterior and interior was locked at all times so, in any given day, a staff member would lock and unlock doors dozens of times. And once in a while, a patient, drawn by the brightly colored buttons, pushed the alarms but the resulting pandemonium was short lived as multiple phone calls were made, in relay, to cancel any response.

Stan and Matt arrived first from the second floor and approached the crouching patient. It only took a few minutes for them to convince him to walk quietly to his room for a "time out."

Looking up at the two huge men quickly convinced him. Dwayne may have been impulsive and angry but he wasn't stupid. Any resistence would result in being escorted to the locked Seclusion Room, usually accompanied by a strong sedative. But he still managed to land a punch on Matt's arm as they escorted him down the hall.

"Ya know, they don't pay me enough to take this shit!" Mat continued to rub his arm.

"Man, stop bitchin'!You just mad cuz ol' Dwayne sucker punched you!" laughed Stan" You gettin old, man!" Laughing as well, Matt called to the LPN, Margaret." Margaret. Hey woman! I think Dwayne's ready for his "cocktail!"

"I'm coming. Hold your horses, Jeez Louise!"

"Yeah, and so is Christmas." smirked Stan.

"You guys just don't have any respect for medicine. Takes a few minutes to find the right mix, I ain't making martinis, ya know! And then I have to "shake and stir. Or is it shaken ?"

Unescorted, she made her way to Dwayne's room. Knowing the drama had ceased, she was confident that Dwayne would pose no further threat to staff or patients.

"You the ugliest skinny white woman I ever saw, Miz Margaret!

Got any smokes?"

"So I'm told," grinned Margaret." And when are you going to give me some new compliments? Try to get some new lines! Everytime you come 'visit' us, you use the same ones. Now, you stop all this crap? I'll give you one at the smoke break."

As Margaret attended Dwayne, Kay, Pat and Deenie assisted Dr. Sanchez. He seemed to be bleeding from his nose but it didn't appear broken. Enormously swollen and cut from the ridge of his glasses, he looked for all the world that he had been in a fight; and lost.

The three registered nurses kicked into action as Kay took his vital signs; blood pressure, pulse, and respirations. Deenie got out the ice pack and Pat called over to the medical clinic for an ambulance. Although his blood pressure was elevated and his face hurt like hell, he was dismissive of all the attention but still a little pleased.

"Ladies! Please! No ambulance! I'll be OK in a minute or two."

Pat knew he would refuse the ambulance but insisted, " Oh no... we got your back, Dr. Sanchez and you either go by ambulance or we walk you over to the clinic. Choose one, and now."

Sanchez knew better than to challenge his three nurses so he finally agreed to be escorted across the street to the medical clinic. The trip over proved uneventful and Pat kept checking her "patient" for any signs of further distress. Once inside, the physical exam agreed with Pat's assessment: no break but some soft tissue damage and an elevated blood pressure due to stress.

Dr. Johnson, the clinic doctor, inquired, " Are you OK to drive?Cause you are going home, and now. I'll release you to go home but not back to Admissions."

"But I'm..."

"No buts. Home or you stay here and keep me company until I go home at five. And then, I drive you home...get it?"

The psychiatrist knew he was outnumbered. He was in pain and extremely tired but he could still work!There were more patients to attend to and notes to dictate. But finally, he relented to superior might and agreed. He could deal with Johnson but he knew he couldn't fight his nurses too. He wasn't that masochistic!

"And Deenie will follow in her car. I'll drive you. I already called Kay and she has the ward quiet and under control and Matt and Stan will stay until we get back."

Again, Sanchez began to protest.

"And don't argue! How many times have we told you to be careful around these guys?Especially when they're "showing their asses" ?Huh? But noooo...You just gotta jump all in it and everytime!"

Working with these people for years, Dr. Johnson stepped back and laughed at the lecture being directed to the psychiatrist. Sanchez's team were well known as a loyal, tight knit group as well as for their expertise.

Pat's chiding was half hearted as she knew that such warnings were falling on deaf ears. Dr. Sanchez would continue "jumping all in it" as long as he could be of assistance and everyone knew it. But what had really rattled them was that this was the first they had ever seen "their doc" attacked and injured and the whole experience had greatly upset them.

"OK...I'll go home for the time being but I'll be back tomorrow."

"Not so fast, Doctor! I'm the Attending physician here, not you! Remember? You're out of your jurisdiction and you're in my clinic. I'm the chief hombre here! No deal. I won't medically clear you to go back to Admissions for at least two days. And if and I mean if you do as you are told and you're feeling better, then you can return."

"I'm sure I'll be fine by tomorrow."

"Day after tomorrow...forty eight hours. What! You trying to get me fired?Think about it! What would you do if our roles were reversed?"

"All right. You made your point."

Handing Sanchez two little pills. he directed, " Now, you go home and take these for relaxation. And stop looking at me like I have horns! I just gave you two and I want to make sure you rest and if I have to medicate you, by God, I will! Now, you can stand here all day but I'd stop arguing, man!"

The psychiatrist knew he had exhausted all his options and knew Johnson was right. The smart and logical thing to do would be to rest and let his face, as well as his pride recover. Left to his own devices, he would have returned to the wards to finish his work and he knew that by agreeing to come to the clinic, he had surrendered some control as to treatment. He reluctantly agreed.

The two doctors had worked together for many years and shared a liking and respect for one another and Johnson could trust that Manolo would comply with treatment. As they left the clinic, Johnson put his hand on Manolo's shoulder and laughed.

"Jeez, Manuel. For a guy that's looking at retirement in a few months, You sure are stubborn!"

Driving Sanchez home, Pat had suggested they stop for groceries but the doctor assured her there was no need. Finally arriving at his condominium with Deenie following behind, the nurses ushered him safely inside. Once they had ascertained for themselves that he did have provisions, they reluctantly left the man to some peace and quiet...but under protest.

"Funny how a simple punch could cause all that uproar!" He pondered. "My Lord, they don't have any idea what real violence is!"

Suddenly he felt very tired as his face began to throb. "Just a delayed reaction to the stress. My parasympathetic system is starting to kick in. I'll just grab some milk and a few donuts and some aspirin." As he walked over to the sofa, he caught sight of the two tiny pills and remembered his promise to be compliant with treatment. And between the aspirin and the sedatives, he began to relax and feel drowsy.

Chuckling to himself, he thought, " How many times have I cautioned patients to be compliant with treatment? I guess it's time to practice what I preach!" He lay on the couch thinking, " My goodness! these damn things work quickly!" And yawning, said to himself, " At least I can sleep for awhile and later I'll call Jaime and see what's new in Spain."

"The object of Life is not to be on the side of the majority but to escape finding oneself in the realm of the insane."

Marcus Aurelius

Chapter Twenty Tthree

Leaving his visit with Morpheo, Sanchez barely heard the ringing. Phone? Doorbell?He glanced at the wall clock, dismayed that it was eleven am. " Jesus, I've been on the couch for nearly twenty four hours." His head clearing, he focused on the sound. Someone was leaning on his doorbell. Making his way to the door and painfully aware of his full bladder, he was shocked to find Bill, the hospital's Chief of Security.

"You OK, Doc?Your girls are really worried.They've been calling you every hour now and getting no answer. Kay finally asked, or I should say, told me to get my ass over here and check on you. Laughing, he added, " So here I am...I ain't gonna mess with them."

"I'm fine, Bill. Sorry to have troubled you! Dr. Johnson gave me some pills to help me sleep and they really kicked in."

"Maybe now you know how that crap works! I've seen that shit knock a grown man flat on his ass and right quick!"

Sanchez agreed, " Thanks again, I'll call the ward and let them know I'm Ok and who'll be covering until I come in tomorrow. I'll call Dr. G. now." Shaking hands in departure, Bill left the still groggy doctor.

Her colleagues could read her like a book and Kay 's facial expression and body language conveyed trouble, big trouble. "He's still not answering the damn phone! I'm calling Security right now. Bill needs to get his ass over there."

Any one of the three team nurses would have gone to Dr. Sanchez's condo to check on him but for a slight problem: There were three new admissions and the wards were all war zones. There were precious few staff as it was and even a thirty minute absence from the building, from any staff, could prove disasterous. It was already two pm and none of them had been able to stop for lunch, with a patient in seclusion on each ward, among other crises. It was just one of those "Days from Hell."

"What a hell of a day to get a new supervisor, eh ladies?" In all the melee, Deenie and Kay had forgotten that this was the day the new Admissions supervisor was to begin. All the staff were eager to meet the new woman as rumors of her hire were flying fast and furious and not much was of a complimentary nature. Administration had informed them only of her name: Kate Wingfield.

No one had met her and given past supervisors, they weren't expecting much. "I just called Bill and he's going right over to Dr. Sanchez and he alerted the fire department just in case they can't get in, and he's got his two way radio and will let us know..." She had finally run out of breath.

Comfortable that Bill had taken charge, the nurses returned to their chaos. They had finally started to restore some sort of order when they saw Mr. Foster coming into the building and he wasn't alone.

The three of them all had similiar thoughts. This one will take one look at all this mess and turn right around and leave. Or, she would be just like all the others; talk about teamwork and dedication but stay safely tucked upstairs in her office. They had experienced that attitude too often and expected more of the same.

"Well ladies, here is your new boss. And she comes to us all the way from Boston! Harvard trained, as well! Kate Wingfield, this is Pat, Kay & Deenie. They're your best nurses and know all the ropes and they'll help you get settled in."

Introductions and nicities over, Mr. Foster guided the new supervisor toward the door." Gotta show her her office. Bye!" Watching the two walk down the hall, the three laughed." I give her a week," Deenie predicted.

"Naw...a month, but no more," countered Kay. "Well, she looks OK.... but a redhead ?"

Matt sauntered off the ward into the staff station, " Hey, who is the goodlookin' redhead? Kinda cute, but no ass. And man she is some white! She one of those albinos or somethin'?"

"Matt, you get your trifing ass back on that unit. And for your information, that's our new boss. Now git!" Deenie playfully attempted to push Matt toward the door but it was like trying to move a refrigerator...with a head.

"And you know what they say about redheads!"

Perplexed, Matt was paying close attention to the trio." What? I ain't never knowed no redheads before."

"Hell, they're something. They tend to be high strung."

"Yeah, and bad tempered, mean as snakes!"

"Just don't piss her off. She'll stick you on night shift and permanently!"

Hurrying back to the ward, all he could say was, " Damn!"

The three RNs all doubled over in laughter. Once they got control of themselves, Pat gave voice to their collective thoughts. They were only teasing Matt and but privately wondered if any of those things were true of the new woman.

Pat was last with her assessment, " I say she'll keep going right out that door!" But, to their collective amazement, they were all wrong. Twenty minutes later, Bill called from Security. Pat picked up the call.

"Dr. Sanchez is fine. He just was sleeping so hard he didn't hear the phone or the door." Giggling, Bill continued, " So me and the boys used the bullhorn. By God that would wake the dead and it sure did.. He says he'll be back tomorrow and to call Dr. G. if you need anything; he's covering." Still giggling like a fool, Bill hung up.

Pat lost no time in letting all the staff know about their "Doc" . Now they could relax and focus more on the patients but it continued to be a battle. What they needed was more staff, just some more bodies on their side of the skirmish.

Everyone was surprised when a few moments later, their new supervisor entered the ward." Looks like it's pretty hectic!So, what can I do to help you ?"

"But you just got here. You probably have lots of paperwork and all."

"Kay, isn't it? And Deenie and Pat? Look, I may be in charge, but I'm new here. You guys know the deal. And I may be in the South now but people are always more important than paperwork, so you guys tell me how I can help."

Pleasantly surprised, they lost no time assigning her tasks. It wasn't long before they were all finally able to take a short break, having caught up with all the work.

"OK now? If things are stable, I'll go finish making rounds. But page me if you need me. I'll be here for several more hours."

As Kate took the stairs to the second floor, the first floor staff began to wonder:Just who this Wingfield woman? It was unheard of for an administrator to actually work with patients!Their experience had shown them to expect little from their supervisors other than more work assignments and criticism. Most of the first floor staff were in agreement; Wingfield was just beginning. She would soon become like all the others and spend her days barking out orders from her office.

The next morning, Dr. Sanchez hurried to work. Morning staff meetings had begun but as he was still tired from the medication, he was running late.

Everyone inquired about his health, the females hovering a bit like mother hens.

"Honestly, I'm feeling fine, My nose hurts a little, but not as much as my pride. And to quote Bill, that sedative really" kicked my ass"

The others smiled in amazement to hear Dr. Sanchez use such language. In all their years working with him, no one could recall him using any profanity, not once.

"OK, now to the wards."

Since Dr. Sanchez had been gone a mere two days, Dwayne was unwittingly driving staff and fellow patients to distraction. He was obsessing about the psychiatrist as he paced back and forth all the while pounding on the ward door demanding to see Sanchez.

It was getting so bad that the Treatment Team worried about his upcoming discharge. He was so close but his increased anxiety could present a barrier. In spite of almost constant reassurance by everyone that Dr. Sanchez was just taking a few days for much needed rest, Dwayne could not relax. And his repetative words were becoming almost a chant...another psychiatric concern.

"I'm good...it's all good.. I jes want to see him and 'pologize, thas all.Why he ain't here? I didn't hurt 'im that bad!"

Dwayne was the first to see the psychiatrist walk toward the ward. His window banging became deafening and at first, the staff thought some sort of crisis had occurred but as they turned around to see what the patient was pointing at, the psychiatrist entered the staff station. Dwayne's behavior continued to escalate.

"Man, it's great to see you, Doc! But I think you need to go see your patient first. He's been driving us nuts since he hit you."

"Great to be back! But no, Mr. Dwayne needs to learn some patience. We can't continue to immediately respond to every need. His family has done that and look at the mess. No, I'll acknowlege him but let him know I'll come talk to him after I make rounds. We have many other patients that need attention."

Sanchez smiled and waved at Dwayne as Pat let herself onto the ward. But before she could close the door behind, Dwayne had slipped through, was off the ward and standing in front of the psychiatrist. Deenie and Kay quickly circled them both.

"Hey man, I's sorry, really, man...you OK? I didn't break nuthin, did I ? Hey man. I jus loss control...Ok, man?We cool?"

Sanchez signaled the nurses that everything was under control." I'm OK, but you have to follow treatment and being off the ward is not part of it."

"But man, I had to see you and.. and..'pologize an all."

Calm and continuing to smile, Sanchez responded, " I understand that and yes, I accept your apology but you must go back to the ward now. I 'll come see you later today. I've got lots of things to take care of. Now, off you go!"

Deenie took his hand and directed him onto the ward. As the door was closing, Dwayne yelled, "You promise, man?"

"Absolutely!"

"Well, that was some welcome back but a simple hello would have done just as well." Finally relaxed, everyone laughed.

"So what did I miss? Anything?"

"Nah.... same old same old; all your patients are stable and Dwayne just being Dwayne."

"But we have a new Admissions Supervisor. Did you meet her yet?"

"Haven't had the pleasure yet. So, think she'll be good to you ladies?"

"Way too early to tell, Doc. But she's not a Southern gal, that's for sure. Funny accent and everything, " Pat answered. Kay and Deenie added their two cents worth.

"Sure as hell not Southern, from Bah-stin, as she told us"

"Not bad looking, but red hair and freckles! Kinda like Orphan Annie!"

The visual each imagined cracked them all up. This was going to get very interesting.

Next day, Kate was in the Admissions Building by six thirty am. There were three shifts covering twenty-four hours, and she was determined to meet as many of her staff as possible. Having been a psychotherapist for many years, she was aware of the positive power of "hands on" supervision and wanted to get off to a good start. There was so much to learn, not only about her new job and the hospital, but of Southern culture and all of the idiosyncrocies. Her first challenge had been the new accents. A Boston native, her ear was tuned to the different New England accents but not to those of the South.

"I hate to keep asking them to repeat themselves. They must think I'm hard of hearing but I really don't get it sometimes!" An earlier incident had left her and the staff laughing at one of her misunderstandings.

One of the evening nurses, Donny, hailed from the North Carolina mountains and her thick, regional accent drew comments, mostly playful, from the others. Comments about her drawl were met, in kind, with sarcasm and retorts but mostly were well tolerated. The constant ribbing occasionally ended with some well worn histronics as Donny would wail, " I work and I work, but does anybody really cay-ya?" That was the signal to end all jest and give the nurse a very wide berth.

Early on, Kate had decided to do some of the necessary paperwork and documentation required by the goverment in the staff station instead of in her office. She had started the habit believing she could better assess the Unit's needs and issues while being available, should the inevitable crisis arise.

Making her last rounds, she entered the male ward to get the evening report from Charge Nurse Donny. Struggling to get all the data, Kate thanked the RN and turned to leave. Donny called after her." Codado!"

"Excuse me?"

"Co-da-do."

"I'm sorry Donny, what did you say?"

Frustrated, Donny 's voice began to rise," CLO-DA-DO! CLO-DA-DO!"

Totally embarrassed and still not understanding, Wingfield walked back to the nurse." I really don't understand. Could you show me?" Perhaps she was referring to a new patient but checking her roster, there was no Mr. Clodado.

Donny couldn't believe it. Her new boss was either deaf, dumb as a rock, or both." Miz Wingfield.... I asked you to clo-da-do... on your way out. I already called maintenace 'bout it. It's stickin' and won't lock proper."

"Oh my God, Donny, you were telling me to "close the door!" I really feel embarrassed...I'm so sorry." Kate's face was a deep red as even the patients were amused." You must think I'm really stupid!" she laughed. Donny remained silent but one of the Substance Abuse patients erupted.

"Lady, you is something. All you folks up in Boston dumb as shit?"

Kate had to agree. She had acted pretty dense and even she could see the the humor." No sir, just me. But I catch on pretty quickly!"

As she exited the ward, she could barely hear Donny's words." Jesus, I hope to God she does or else we'll all be in the toilet."

"You should listen to your heart, not the voices in your head."

Matt **Groening**

Chapter Twenty Four

Wingfield had been at work for a few days before she was able to meet all of the staff. She had met most of the doctors, psychologists, social workers, and of course, the nurses. She had even spent some time with Rachel, the activities manager and discovered that she could sink basketballs better than most of the patients. Pretty good for a white girl.

Somehow, it wasn't until a week later that she met Dr. Sanchez. It was not a stellar beginning. As was her routine, she went directly to the wards for a quick morning rounds before she landed in her second floor office. That meant lugging her briefcase around but the time saving method had proven successful. More than once, her" early warning system" had caught a potential problem ready to explode into an "incident." The nurses were getting used to her habits and were slowly warming to their supervisor. She was proving to be true to her word; spending as much time helping on the wards as she did completing administrative responsibilities displaying leadership by example.

Placing her briefcase on a staff station desk, she began to access the computer for the daily Twenty Four Hour Report. As she reviewed the report, she could hear that someone new had entered the staff station.

"Good morning ladies!"

"Mornin Doc!" Busy with early morning diabetic testing and lab draws, the nurses all left for the wards. The man and Kate were alone.

Approaching Wingfield's briefcase, Sanchez noticed a book half- tucked within. A voracious reader, Kate always carried one or two books around for any rare breaks or down time; her latest book by a favorite author Thomas Moore, dealt with the interplay of psychology and spirituality.

As he picked up her book, Dr. Sanchez smiled, "Tell me. Do you really understand any of this?"

"What? For your information, I certainly do." Kate was furious. Who was this insolent and insulting man? Used to being underestimated for most of her life, she had developed a thick skin over the years but once in awhile a zinger got through and hit it's mark. Just at that moment, the three RNs returned to the station to hear:

"And just who the Hell might you be?"

Sanchez stood his ground as he thought that this must be the new supervisor. Attractive, very, but such a temper!

"I'm sorry, I'm forgetting my manners. We haven't met. I'm Manuel Sanchez; one of the psychiatrists."

He had pronounced his name in the proper Spanish; the "z" having a "th" sound. The result sounded like: Sanche-th.

"Ms Wingfield's the new supervisor we told you about." Pat was trying to break the obvious tension.

"I wasn't trying to insult you! It's just that I don't know many people who are actually interested in the subject. I just finished that book and it's wonderful."

Kate extended her hand as she introduced herself. She was still upset but had begun to accept his apology. He certainly appeared to be a gentleman and she liked his manner. So this was the famous Dr. Sanchez that the nurses were always talking about.

Sanchez walked back to his office leaving the women. Deenie was the first to speak, "But Ms Wingfield, that's Dr. Sanchez!He's really a doll once you get to know him."

"Well, he better mind his manners. Questioning my intelligence before we even meet? Bloody hell..."

"But he apologized! And I really think he was flirting with you. You wait. You'll see what a great guy he is."

"Flirting?What kind of idiot flirts with someone by insulting them? "

Still miffed but thawing, Kate looked at the three RNs. "Well, maybe, and I should have more compassion. You didn't tell me he had a speech impediment."

Confused, they responded. A speech impediment? What speech impediment?What are you talking about?He doesn't have any impediment!"

"Sure he does; a lisp! Didn't you hear how he pronounced his name? He ended it with a clear "th" sound...an obvious lisp!"

The area erupted in laughter as the three sat in the chairs. They could barely get a word in. "OMIGOD. You're so funny." Now it was Wingfield's turn to be confused. The RNs began to explain the differences in word pronounciation between English and Spanish. Realizing her misunderstanding, Kate also joined in the joke.

Returning to her office, she mused. "I'm doing just great...the thing with Sanche-th...with Donny...Bloody hell...They must think I'm a real nut case."

Several weeks went by without any major incidents. The more she worked with Dr. Sanchez, the more she found herself liking the man. She respected his medical skills along with his gentle manner with patients and staff. And he seemed to enjoy her company. Often he would seek her out for a quick discussion of some article he had read or to simply chat about treatments, whatever. She soon looked forward to his conversations. This doctor was a little different. He had many intellectual interests and seemed to have studied well, for rarely was a conversation about medicine; usually history, world religions, or cultures. As their medical work was intense and emotionally and physically exhausting, she looked forward to the wonderful respite. She was glad that they were becoming friends.

Wingfield had been at the hospital for almost six months, and even she was amazed at her progress. Gradually, she had earned the respect and trust of most of the staff but as in any situation, there were those who held on to their resentments and distrust. But at least they were vocal about those.

She knew who "had her back" and who did not, so complaints or "poison pen letters" were easy to track and she decided to patiently listen to all concerns and just do her best to address them. Her job was already proving Herculean but she had to admit it was exciting and she was certainly was never bored!

Two weeks before Christmas, influenza hit the Admissions Building affecting both patients and staff. Already at minimum staffing levels, the wards were left in a crucial position. The building was operating at dangerously low staffing levels; one staff per eight acutely mentally ill patients and no matter how many times Kate requested more staff, the Administration denied any increases.

She understood budget concerns but what was so difficult at understanding that Admissions patients were more volatile and dangerous than the well medicated long term units? It just didn't make any sense. She was instructed to 'do her best'. But what if her best wasn't good enough and someone got injured?

There was only one thing to do. She would fill in on the ward as much as possible until the crisis blew over or she became ill, whichever came first.

"Ms Wingfield.What are you doing here?It's after five and you should be leaving. "

"Nope. You have me for a few hours, at least until the patients settle down for the night. So, which ward needs help?" Grateful for another pair of hands, she was directed onto a ward to help with dinner trays and showers.

Things were running smoothly until she heard a commotion in the staff station.

"I told you!That girl's crazy. I don't care about any damn cake! It's a real shame that some folks are so stupid and insensitive."

Coming off the ward, Kate was surprised to see it was Elois. One of the best psychiatric aids, Elois was well liked and respected by all. She was a powerhouse, physically and mentally, and few people would challenge her. All of five feet tall, she had a commanding presence. Patients and staff adored her and trusted her clinical judgement.

"Elois. Why are your knickers in a twist ?"

Aide and supervisor had formed a close working relationship and over the months could usually read each other pretty well. Wingfield was at a loss on this one.

"That trifling Doris, that's what. Come on! I'll show you."

Elois led Kate up the stairs to the second floor staff station. In the middle of the desk was a large cake, ice cream and all the accoutrements for some sort of celebration. It was obvious that someone had gone to alot of trouble judging from the professional job.

"Miss Wingfield. I heard you were still here. Have some cake and ice cream!" Doris got busy slicing. "Miss Elois?"

"Read what's on that damn cake!And Hell no, I ain't having any Confederate cake! And you!" She pointed at Matt and Stan, " You two are just as ignorant!" With that, off stormed Elois back downstairs.

Why would anybody be upset at a cake? Kate began to read the cake's icing. Beautifully scrolled was Happy 100th Birthday General Pickett. Who? Who in Hell is General Pickett? Kate wisely refused the treats claiming to be dieting but she was very curious why a cake should be so upsetting.

"I'm wondering, Doris...I really don't have any idea of who Pickett is."

"Nooooooooo.. don't get her started." Stan and Matt pleaded with Wingfield. We've heard this a million times before, not again!" Groaning, they returned to the ward leaving Doris with a new 'victim.'

Doris was delighted to retell the life of her favorite dead person: General George Pickett. With a rapturous look, she began the tale.

"A native Virginian, General George Pickett was one of General Lee's Confederate leaders during the American Civil War. He graduated from West Point with a commision in the US. Army and served with honors in the war with Mexico, between 1847-48. But when the Civil War broke out, he resigned his commission and joined those brave boys in the Confederacy. He's best known for the last great charge at Gettsyburg where he valiantly led a division telling his men, "Up to your posts, men!Don't forget you are from Old Virginia!" And that is famously known as Pickett's Charge. But it was really partly General Lee's fault, you know, demanding more and all poor George could say was, "General, I have no division." And..." Kate's eyes were beginning to glaze over as Doris droned on.

"He was pardoned by President Grant. And he married the prettiest gal in Virginia, LaSalle Corbell. And he's buried in Richmond and...."

Stan and Matt timed it perfectly and returned to the staff station. Someone had to rescue poor Ms Wingfield from Doris's clutches! "Hey Doris! Lecture over yet?"

Seizing her chance for escape, Kate quickly added, "Such fascinating stuff, Doris but I really need to go make rounds."

"But, I just told you the highlights! There's so much more of this honorable man's life that you should know!"

"Ms Wingfield, did she get to the part about the loser being last in his class?Or that he lost over half of his division?Or that he ran to Canada after the war?"

Stan continued. "How about that the old goat was almost forty when he married the chick.His third wife by the way, and she was just a teenager!"

"Or how about that he ended up in Richmond, selling insurance for a New York company? An insurance man. Right...some hero."

Ignoring the comments, Doris continued," So every year on his birthday, I celebrate! And since I had to come to work this evening, I thought I'd share my celebration. Besides, he really does appreciates it."

Wingfield blinked, "He appreciates it ?" Looking directly at Doris, she asked,"Who exactly is "he?"

Matt piped up," Oh Doris here, she does that thing where she dresses up and pretends she's fighting the Yankees. You know, at Gettysburg, places like that."

"Matt, I keep telling you, it's called "Re-enactment."

"Yeah, re-enactment. And she says Pickett talks to her!" Unable to keep his serious demeanor any longer, Matt burst out laughing.

Doris continued to explain,"You see, I have a powerful connection to George; General Pickering. It's spiritual and sometimes I feel his presence, his spirit, especially on the battlefield."

"Hey Doris! Bet ya'd like to feel him in other ways."

Doris cast a disapproving look at Matt." Go ahead! Make fun! You're all acting evil. Just evil!"

"Aw, Doris, you know we love ya.Ya may be crazy as a shithouse rat but we love ya!" Stan seemed to placate the nurse. Smiling again, Doris turned toward Kate.

"Thanks for the offer Doris, and the fascinating story. Now please, try to keep the ward and the staff quiet, OK?" She had a feeling she would not hear the end of this saga. Kate seized her opportunity and exited the area.

In a work environment staffed by mostly Southern African Americans, what in Hell was Doris thinking?Kate could see no obvious evidence of malicious intent. Perhaps she simply didn't think; made a massive, insensitive error in judgement. But even if that were the case, Kate shuddered to think what other bonehead decisions were being made without her knowledge?.

Kate had been at SSH a relatively short time but in that time, she had met several "Doris types." Unsettling. And how many more were there? "Now, I get what Kay was talking about, that some staff were "patients with the keys! "

"The Journey, not the arrival matters."
T. S. Eliot

Chapter Twenty Five

It was the week before Christmas and in spite of the mild temperatures hovering around fifty degrees, everyone in Admissions was in good spirits.

Christmas carols were being sung throughout the building by staff and patients alike and Rachel, whose wonderful alto voice led the singing, adding her special greetings of Merry 'Hanukkamus'. For a rare moment, " Goodwill" truly was in the air.

It was Kate's first Christmas in the South and she found she was enjoying herself. Sure, there wasn't any snow but aside from that, everything felt familiar.

Besides, she certainly didn't miss all that shoveling and constant cold! In high spirits, she felt truly peaceful and happy most of the time. Her job continued to present daily challenges but all the other facets of her life were going smoothly.

She had made some good friends, loved her garden and home and finally decided that she had indeed, made the right decision to move South. She felt she was truly Home.

Geographical changes do not neccesitate personality changes so she would continue her own traditions. In Boston, it was usual for most hospital staff to give a small gift to one another during the holiday season. She didn't know what the custom was here at SSH, so she asked the only person she knew who would give her a straight answer: Miss Elois.

"So, tell me what you guys do around here at Christmas."

"You mean besides working our tails off and spending most of it with the patients instead of being home with our families?"

Elois smiled, but she had to add the truth to her answer. She had worked with Wingfield for close to a year and a deep, personal relationship had developed between the two based on mutual respect and caring. Elois could count on her boss to make her laugh with her positive attitude.

Elois would often tell her, "Wingfield, I ain't seen nothing like it! You could walk into a room piled high with horse shit and be looking for a shovel all the while saying, "Gotta be a pony around here somewhere!" And no matter how often she repeated the joke, it drew a smile from both.

"No, I mean, does anyone give gifts? I mean, you know...like to each other? I haven't seen anything in the SOP (Standards of Operating Procedure) about it and I thought if anyone would know, you would. I'm aware that the hospital gives the patients presents, but what does the staff do to celebrate?"

"Miss Wingfield, have you done lost your mind? Don't they have Christ- mas in Bah-stin? You're still in America, you know!" Elois chuckled, "Seriously, we usually have a small staff party and people exchange gifts; to people we like."

With a twinkle in her eye, Kate couldn't resist, "Like Doris?"

"That trifling piece of...don't get me started...I'm trying to be Christian about that...that...crazy heathen!"

Armed with her information, Kate made a list of her staff that she wanted to remember with a holiday gift. She would continue her practice of choosing a gift that was appropriate, not too expensive and somewhat personalized.

Her nurses were easy to buy for except for Leo, her best (and only) male nurse. But she would figure that out later. Deciding to buy a very good bottle of wine for each of the three doctors was also a breeze. From previous conversations, Drs. G. and Johnson favored a French Burgundy but what about Dr. Sanchez? Obviously, only a good Spanish Rioja would suffice.

The Friday before the holiday weekend, she took advantage of her position. As Admissions supervisor, she carried keys to every door in the building. Safety dictated that only a handful of employees had access keys as any key falling into the wrong hand could result in theft or worse; patient escapes.

She spent the next few hours surreptitiously playing Santa, leaving Sanchez until last. Finally seeing him leave for lunch, she found her opportunity and entered his office and leaving the gift and card, she quietly left.

Upon returning from lunch, Sanchez was very surprised to find the gift waiting. He opened the card and read: Merry Christmas from Kate. He then opened the large box to find the Rioja. But how did she...? Since living alone, he had looked at the Christmas season with a jaundiced eye. True, he faithfully made generous monetary gifts to his two sons for their families each year aware that growing families like theirs could always use extra financial assistance, especially around this time. They were much better at picking out what everyone really wanted than he. And he did take some plea sure knowing his grandchildren would receive something special from "Abuelo."

Always a man of simple tastes, he preferred more sedate celebrations, a good book, maybe with a glass of wine. Let the younger folks do the celebrating.

Although pleased, he wasn't sure how to respond. Perhaps Kate had suspected his attraction to her and was opening a door to a deeper relationship? No, that was dreaming, just fantasy, she was much younger than he. Why would someone like her even consider something like that? Impossible!

But, he really liked the woman. Easy to talk with, with shared interests and she did seem to enjoy his company as well. Not to mention his physical attraction and that was unfortunately growing along with strong doubts.

"Nonsense! I'm too old for another affair of the heart. I learned that lesson the hard way. I'm not interested in any casual affair and if that's the only option?Absolutely not, not ever again!" He was growing tired of his emotions vascillating from one extreme to another. "I just don't need this! But then, I feel really good when I'm with her, and alive! Even the staff have noticed that I'm smiling more!I wish I hadn't come back to the hospital. Damn her! And she should have stayed in Boston!" And so it went, back and forth and on and on....

But no matter how conflictual his emotional state, he was aware of his manners and knew he needed to respond. Picking up the phone, he dialed her office only to get her blasted answering machine. Must be on the wards making rounds. One by one, he called each ward only to be told that Ms Wingfield had "just left." His anxiety was increasing but having left instructions for her to call him, all he could do was patiently wait for her call. Any more calls, and the staff would begin to worry or worse, suspect something. This was getting silly! He was feeling like a teenager before a first date. He needed to get control of himself!

Returning to her office, Kate found several notes tacked to her door's message board all asking her to call Dr. Sanchez. Strange? Her anxiety began to filter in as she thought about potential reasons: problems with a patient, with a staff ? Maybe he was angry at the gift. She had bent hospital rules a bit. No alcohol allowed on the hospital campus. Hah! She had seen that rule bent many times. But she had been the model of discretion making sure the wrapping was well disguised. But it would be extremely embarrassing, to say the least, to be caught with contraband in her position.

Listening to her messages, she responded to the critical ones first, as daily "fires" always needed quenching. Finally, she called Sanchez's office.

"Hi. It's Kate. Are you looking for me?"

"Oh Hello! Yes. I'm wondering if you could come down to my office. I need to speak with you."

"Sure, I'll be there in about ten minutes...OK?"

"Fine. See you then."

Damn! The psychiatrist sounded strange; too formal. She began to feel uncomfortable. Perhaps her gift was in bad taste after all?" He's probably going to give me a lecture about it. Well, Kate, another idiotic decison...good move. Brilliant, Kate! Simply brilliant!" Reaching Sanchez's office, she continued to mentally disparage herself. After a couple of false starts, she finally knocked on the door.

"Come in. It's not locked."

Watching her enter his office, the doctor was again struck by his attraction to her. " I just wanted to thank you for the wonderful gift! I don't find many wines from Spain around here and it's one of my favorites!"

Flooded with relief, Kate beamed with pleasure. He wasn't upset with her after all! She suddenly realised just how much his opinion of her mattered. Where did this come from? My goodness! And she was blushing!

"I'm so glad you liked it. I was afraid you might not and I wanted to give you something special; something that you'd enjoy. I really value our relationship, you know. We work well together and have become good friends and all..."

Moving towards her, he gently asked, "May I give you a hug ?"

"Of course! I'd like that!" As they embraced, Kate felt wonderful. It had been a long time, indeed, since she had enjoyed being in the arms of an attractive man.

Manuel gently enveloped her. "My God she feels terrific! So warm, soft, and what a sensuous perfume." Shaking himself back to the moment, he looked and smiled at her upturned face. " You know, if I were a hundred years younger you'd be in serious trouble."

The embrace ending, Kate found herself blushing again. In her embarrassment, she playfully grabbed his nose and turned to leave. Smiling, she was a loss for words but thought, " Oh, but my dear Dr. Sanchez, you don't realize that it's much too late! I already am in serious trouble!"

Not Quite The End

"We shall not cease from exploration. And the end of all our explorings will be to arrive where we started and know the place for the first time."
T. S. Eliot

Internationale

("Red" anthem)

Aribba parias de la Tierre	Arise ye wretched from your slumber
En pie famelica legion!	Arise ye convicts of hunger
Atruena la razon en marcha	For reason in revolt now thunders
Es fin de la opresion	And ends at last the age of can't.
Agrupemonos todos	So comrades come rally
En la lucha final	To fight the last fight
El genero humano	Let us form the Internationals
Es la Internationales	Unites the human race!

Cara al Sol

("White" anthem)

Cara al sol con la camisa nueva	Facing the sun in my new shirt
Que tu bordaste en rojo ayer yesterday	That you embroidered in red
Me hallara la muerte si me lleva	That's how death will find me if it takes me
Yo no te vuelvo a ver	And I won't see you again.
España una.	Spain United.
España grande.	Spain the Great.
España grande.	Spain the Free.
Arriba España	Onwards Spain.

ABOUT THE AUTHOR

Born in Boston,Massachusetts, Katheryn Lovell began her professional life as a Psychiatric Registered Nurse. Subsequently, she maintained a successful private practice in psychotherapy,after graduate school, for nearly thirteen years. She is currently an adjunct Professor of Psychology at Thomas Nelson Community College where she amuses her students as she attempts to educate them.

An unrepentant "foodie" and wine afficianado" (or wino, depending on one's perspective), she enjoys combining the two with good company.She and her husband Manuel,happily reside in Williamsburg,Virginia. Between them they have five adult children who have managed to create good lives for themselves in spite of their "shrink"parents.

CPSIA information can be obtained at www.ICGtesting.com
Printed in the USA
BVOW02s1827030516

446594BV00001B/29/P